PANTHER GLADE

PANTHER GLADE

HELEN CAVANAGH

SIMON & SCHUSTER
BOOKS FOR YOUNG READERS
Published by Simon & Schuster
New York • London • Toronto • Sydney • Tokyo • Singapore

SIMON & SCHUSTER BOOKS FOR YOUNG READERS
Simon & Schuster Building, Rockefeller Center
1230 Avenue of the Americas
New York, New York 10020
Copyright © 1993 by Helen Cavanagh
All rights reserved including the right of
reproduction in whole or in part in any form.
SIMON & SCHUSTER BOOKS FOR YOUNG READERS
is a trademark of Simon & Schuster.
Designed by David Neuhaus.
Manufactured in the United States of America
10 9 8 7 6 5 4 3 2 1

Library of Congress Cataloging-in-Publication Data
Cavanagh, Helen.
Panther glade / by Helen Cavanagh.
          p.   cm.
Summary: Bill gains self-confidence when he spends the summer in
Florida with Aunt Cait, an archaeologist studying the ancient
Calusa Indians.
[1. Great-aunts—Fiction.   2. Self-confidence—Fiction.   3. Calusa
Indians—Antiquities—Fiction.   4. Indians of North America—
Florida—Antiquities—Fiction.   5. Florida—Fiction.]   I. Title.
PZ7.C2774Pan   1993
[Fic]—dc20   92-23406   CIP   ISBN: 0–671–75617–6

To my dear sister, Marrie Farrenkopf,
who shared her island paradise, so sure
I was meant to spin out the story of
the Key Marco Cat-god

And to my husband, Larry, whose love
and support helped to make all my
story spinnings possible

Acknowledgments

Heartfelt appreciation to my hunch-playing, hard-working agent, Jim Roginski, and to my much-esteemed editor, Olga Litowinsky, who taught me how. Thank you both for believing in me.

And I also want to give thanks to Cary Ryan, for helping; my wonderful family, for waiting; Bill Soriano, for being you; Shelly Soriano and Marie Tracy, for the loan of your amazing Virgo minds; Donna Fletcher, Suzanne Hoos, Johnnie Ryan-Evans, Kaye Gilmartin, Helen Haney, Ceil Ostapiej, Prudy Taylor, Bonnie Buck, Mark Charde, Bob Dowd, for your enthusiastic support; the *Marco Island Eagle*, for all the great articles about the Calusas, the cat-god, and the locale; *Gulfshore Life*, for information and "atmosphere"; the Art League of Marco Island, with special mention for artist Dick Kramer, for inspiration; the Calusa Constituency, and to everyone working to preserve the past for the future, for caring; Arlene and Wayne Margarum of the Collier House, for dreaming and doing; Ronto Developments Marco, for remembering The Island That Time Forgot.

And grateful acknowledgment to James P. McMullen, courageous crusader for the endangered Florida panther, whose book, *Cry of the Panther* (McGraw-Hill, 1984), was a major source of information and inspiration; to Adrian Malone, whose novel, *The Secret* (Guild Press, 1984), inspired my vision quest scenes; and to Marjory Stoneman Douglas for her definitive book, *The Everglades: River of Grass* (Mockingbird Books, 1974).

Contents

Ever shining, ever bright,
Glade of green and silver light;
Golden, watchful eyes glint out:
I see, he says, I hear—I wait.

Close behind the gate, the king, the cat of old,
Stand bold, unbowed, spirits rising to the sun,
Grand and wise, free and wild:
Oh, I know, he cries, now I see—
This ancient ever-shining glade, this golden sun,
This mighty king, this fierce-proud cat
Is me!
—H. C.

Then the gates of his heart were flung open and
his joy flew far over the sea. And he closed his
eyes and prayed in the silences of his soul.
—Kahlil Gibran, *The Prophet*

1.

Surrounded

"Billy, what *happened*?"

On his hands and knees at the foot of the shell mound, Bill stared straight ahead at Aunt Cait's kneecap. "Up there," he whispered, "on the path."

"What was on the path?" For the first time since he'd met Aunt Cait three days ago, she sounded worried. "Rattler," he said, "a diamondback!"

Looking up, he saw her hands shake as she stripped the wrapping from a stick of gum.

"That's why I was yelling at you to be careful. Rattlers hunt for their supper when the sun goes down, and—oh, Bill—" Her voice shook too, his name ending up as a gargle.

Bill scrambled to his feet, flexed his banged knees, and blew on his bruised palms. "S-sorry, Aunt Cait."

She sighed. "We'll have to have a long talk, you and I."

He followed her to the car. Anything was okay with him now that he was on safe, solid ground. Once Aunt Cait was driving away from Indian Hill, she kept her promise. Except the talk she said she wanted them to have turned out to be a lecture. While he sat scrunched down in the passenger seat watching palm trees sway past his window, she talked.

"I'm considered one of the experts on the culture of the Calusa people," Aunt Cait said, "but I'm certainly not an expert on kids. I'm going to need your cooperation."

Beyond the road, past the trees and flowering shrubs, Bill caught glimpses of the Gulf of Mexico. With the sun almost gone, deep-purple shadows striped the water.

"Until you get used to things around here, will you listen to what I tell you? You've seen what can happen when you don't."

"I promise," he said.

"Good, that's all I ask. This is the subtropics, quite a bit different from New Jersey."

"Right."

"Don't worry, Billy, you'll catch on fast. We're going to have a wonderful summer together. I *know* we are."

But as she drove the few miles across Marco Island to her home, he stayed silent, thinking about the rattler and what could've happened if he hadn't seen it in time. If he'd *stepped* on it.

After two straight days of riding in Aunt Cait's car, cooped up from New Jersey all the way to Florida, he'd been glad when she stopped to show him the shell mound. Charging full speed up Indian Hill had seemed to him the only way to unkink his cramped muscles and get rid of his restlessness. He'd bolted past Aunt Cait, scrambling as fast as he could up the dusty path. Halfway up the hill he'd stopped to catch his breath. That's when he saw it.

Sitting here in Aunt Cait's car, if he closed his eyes, he could still see it. Its body piled up like thick metallic rope, the rattler's head rose slowly, its lidless eyes regarding him coldly. If he tried, Bill could hear again the ominous dry rattling sound. That sound was all he'd needed. He'd turned and barreled down the hill. Skidding, sweating, and gasping for breath, he'd fallen at Aunt Cait's feet—safe.

Bill guessed he would have to watch his step around this awful subtropic island from now on.

Aunt Cait finished her monologue about safety just as they pulled into her driveway. Her house was white with a tin roof and a high railed porch wrapped around it.

"Olde-Florida style," she explained. "Brand-new but old-timey. It's the kind of house early settlers here built."

"Great house," Bill said and got out of the car.

Standing there in the driveway, Aunt Cait clasped her hands together, pressing them up under her chin. She stared straight ahead, as if she were hypnotized.

"The minute I saw this house, I knew I had to have it. Fortunately the builder's a good friend of mine. As the saying goes, he made me an offer I couldn't refuse. Besides, the name of the house was Coquina, after a pretty local shell. How could I resist?"

Bill hoped they would go inside soon. Even with the landscaping lights outlining the driveway and the path leading to the front steps, outdoors was getting darker by the second.

Also, across the road he saw a stretch of dark woods. Not that he hated woods. The woods behind his house in New Jersey were okay, but the animals there were harmless types, squirrels and rabbits and deer. Here? He didn't want to think about it. Right then, more than anything, he wanted to be high off the ground on Aunt Cait's porch. Instead, he had to stand still and act cool while she piled boxes and bags in his arms.

At last she slammed shut the car trunk, loaded her own arms full of luggage, and led the way up the porch steps.

Once he was inside her house, with a couple of lights switched on, Bill set the boxes down and stared around him.

Two walls of the large room were lined with shelves. On the shelves closest to him he saw seashells and starfish, little white statues, and a chunk of driftwood with twisted black roots.

And did Aunt Cait ever have books! Books had practically taken over the place: piled up high on little tables; stacked up under large tables. Towers of books leaned crazily against the sides of strange carved chairs. He wanted to laugh. He could just imagine what his mother would say about this mess.

Seashells knotted on long strings dangled on either side of the arched doorway where Aunt Cait stood. She laughed softly. "Welcome to my world, Billy. Like it?"

"Sure," he said, although he wasn't sure at all. He was worn out from the long trip, and these new surroundings looked pretty weird, more like a museum than a living room.

"These are bits and pieces from all the places I've been. You might say this house is a museum of my memories." She pointed to a pony-sized gold-painted sphinx lounging on the polished floor tiles beyond the rug fringe. "A little bit of Egypt."

She pointed again. "That's a replica of the Mayan calendar, but what you see here is mostly Calusa. I admit it, I'm Calusa crazy. Want to bet you will be too before the summer is over?"

"Maybe," Bill murmured, staring into a big copper bowl filled to the brim with feathers. "What are these, Aunt Cait?"

"Gifts from the Great Spirit," she said. "The ancients believed finding a feather was a good omen, an announcement of something special about to happen. Each and every feather in that bowl is a souvenir of a new friend met, an important discovery, a difficult puzzle solved, special gifts of all kinds."

"Aunt Cait, you sound like you really believe all that stuff about great spirits and good omens. Aren't archaeologists scientists? Aren't scientists supposed to be against things like that?"

"Against? Not me. My mind stays open to every possibility." She pointed across the room. "Look."

Painted masks hung in a triple row on the opposite wall. Life-sized animal, reptile, and human faces stared back at him, their white shell eyes gleaming.

Bill crossed the room for a better look. "Wow, where'd you get all those?"

"Not *those*, Billy," she whispered, "*them*!"

Aunt Cait waved both hands at the masks. "Hello, I'm baaack."

"What are the masks for?" he asked.

"Religious dances and ceremonies. The original masks were discovered here over a hundred years ago. But for heaven's sake, Bill, don't tell them they're only copies." She smiled. "My masks are convinced they're the real thing."

To keep from laughing he pointed at a large framed poster hanging on the wall next to a window. "What's th—" Aunt Cait interrupted him. "Not *what*. In this case, most definitely who. My dear grand-nephew, you now have the high privilege of meeting—ta-dum, ta-dum—our famous Key Marco Cat-god!

"Cat-god," she announced in the same loud, dramatic voice, "meet William Russell Carven, come to visit your ancient paradise island from New Jersey."

"Hi," Bill said before he could stop himself.

"She, or he, as you choose, was discovered right here on Marco Island, which used to be called Key Marco.

I'll tell you the whole story sometime. The original is at the Smithsonian in Washington, D.C., for safekeeping. It's a rare find, from A.D. 600."

"Really?" Looking at the poster made him feel sort of good inside. The cat-god's carved-round eyes, long nose, and straight back, the way its paws rested so calmly on its lap, everything about it looked proud and dignified. Aunt Cait was right, he decided. The Key Marco Cat-god was definitely a who, not a what.

An enlarged color photograph drew him closer. "What—I mean, who's that?"

Aunt Cait was crouched on the floor, thumbing through a book, but she looked up quickly, an expression of pride spreading across her face. "That's our Florida panther."

"Panther? I thought panthers were black."

"Technically it's not a panther, it's a cougar. It's had all kinds of names over the centuries: *catsa, cootota-chobee*, catamount. Spanish explorers thought it was a lion, probably because of the color. Some experts claim only twenty or so are left in the Everglades, others insist there are sixty or more. Either way, Billy, it's not enough."

Kneeling on the couch, Bill reached up and gingerly stroked the panther's fangs. "Thankfully we now have laws to protect panthers," she said, "but it may be too late."

"Too late? You mean it?"

"Our panther is one of the most intelligent creatures on the planet. It'd have to be to have survived so long.

Even so, if we're not careful, it could disappear from the earth forever."

She sighed. "Odds are the panther can't survive much longer. Not against speed-demon drivers and hunters who shoot and steal its prey, or the drying up and shrinking of its Glades habitat."

"Any panthers around here, Aunt Cait?" he asked.

"Whenever there's any new building project going on, there are sightings. Unconfirmed sightings usually."

"Any confirmed sightings on this road?"

"I *wish*," she said. "I'd give my eyeteeth for the pleasure of seeing a panther roaming free. And believe me, Bill, at my age, I don't part with teeth easily. No, to the best of my knowledge, all the sightings have turned out to be bobcats. Plenty of those around."

"Ohh," Bill said. "How big are bobcats?"

"Say, this big." She held her hands apart to show him. "Imagine a house cat, then multiply by three."

Hoisting herself up from the floor, Aunt Cait gave another big yawn. "How's that for a scientific answer? Heavens, I'm tired. Aren't you? Listen, Bill, you make yourself at home while I go upstairs and slip into something loose. I'll come back down, and we'll rustle up something to eat. You must be starving."

"I am," he said. Meeting the rattler on Indian Hill had taken away his appetite. Now, safe in Aunt Cait's house, he couldn't wait to eat.

"Your room is down here next to my study. My bedroom's upstairs. This way we'll both have our privacy."

"Okay," he mumbled. Her room was upstairs? He didn't like the thought of sleeping down here all alone, so close to the dark woods.

While she was upstairs, Bill wandered into every room on the first floor. He counted the light switches he passed, counted windows and doors and, finally, the masks.

Hmmm, he pondered uneasily, *three rows of eight masks make twenty-four. I'll be surrounded*. He already felt that way. At Aunt Cait's house there were too many eyes!

He went into his bedroom and sat on the bed to wait. When Aunt Cait appeared in the doorway a few minutes later, Bill was still sitting on the bed, plucking at the threads of the striped bedspread.

"I forgot to tell you, sheets and towels are in the closet."

"Um . . . don't do beds," he said, lifting his head to see her reaction.

Standing there in her purple nightshirt with the words *Let's Get Metaphysical* written on the front, she smelled of soap and toothpaste. With her short brownish-gray hair all brushed up straight, and her tanned skin all greasy with lotion goop, Bill thought she looked like a roasted oven-stuffer chicken with eyeglasses.

"I mean, I never *had* to do my own bed before."

"C'mon," Aunt Cait said, taking off her glasses and laying them and the book in her hands down on the bare bureau top, "I'll show you."

She didn't just take over and make his bed for him. Aunt Cait actually expected him to work at getting the sheets smooth and even. After demonstrating how to get the corners of the sheets tucked in nice and tight, she pulled them apart, then stood back to let him do it.

It seemed to take ages before he got it right. But when his bed was finally made, it was more his, every brown, white, and blue stripe in perfect alignment, his pajama bottoms waiting beneath the pillow.

"We'll leave here about eight in the morning," Aunt Cait told him. "Get to the dig site on Horr's Island about nine. That's allowing time for egg sandwiches at Stan's Marina. Be sure and wear long pants, and a long-sleeved shirt. And a hat, Bill. You have a hat, I hope?"

He shook his head. "Don't do hats much either."

"Never mind, I'll find one for you. Oh, I can't wait for you to meet Annie," she said, leading the way out of the room. "Annie Stokes is about your age, and I'm sure you two will get along just fine."

Following Aunt Cait across the hallway into the kitchen, Bill made an idiot face at her back. He was glad *she* was so sure because he wasn't.

Bill looked over Aunt Cait's shoulder as she scanned the contents of her refrigerator. There wasn't much to see, only juice, fruit, eggs, bread, and one small chicken—which looked just like Aunt Cait!

Oh, not that she was so plump or funny looking, he thought. Actually she looked too young for an old person of fifty-seven. Except for her wrinkles; she had lots of those.

"Annie's father is in Egypt this summer," she told

him. "Ryan Stokes is digging at one of the world's greatest archaeological sites, on the Giza Plateau."

She was on her tiptoes, her head stuck halfway into a high cupboard, and her voice sounded odd.

"Of course, Annie misses her dad a great deal. Her mother is remarried and lives elsewhere. Her grandmother is staying with her this summer, but having you here will perk her up, I think. She really needs a friend, Billy."

Behind her back Bill rolled his eyes. "Hey, Aunt Cait," he wanted to say, "you think *I* don't?"

But when his great-aunt turned and handed him a loaf of bread and pointed to the toaster, he didn't say a word. He got busy making a big stack of buttered toast.

Bill barely liked normal fruit, and definitely not weird fruit like mangoes and passion fruit. He had to make do with scrambled eggs, toast, juice, and two helpings of raspberry sherbet.

When they'd finished eating, he trailed after Aunt Cait while she locked the doors and turned out the lights, every light but his.

"Good night," she said, retrieving her heavy book and eyeglasses from the top of his bureau. "Sleep well."

"G' night," he mumbled, staring at the bare window-panes. Anyone outside, he thought, could see him plain as day in here at night. Anything too.

Aunt Cait lingered in the doorway. "I'm glad you're here. I like living alone, but it *is* a nice feeling having family in the house."

"That's right," he said.

When she left the room, he quickly shut the door and leaned against it. With both hands he yanked at the short spikes of his fresh haircut until the embarrassed feeling went away.

A minute later Bill crawled between the sheets and turned off the light. He tried to relax. It wasn't easy. For one thing a mosquito kept flying around in his dark room, stopping by his ear every little while to whine: "I vant to suck your blood."

Mosquitoes he knew from home, but he was determined no Marco Island mosquito was going to get *him* the first night out.

The head of his bed had mosquito netting tied back at each side. "More for looks than necessity," Aunt Cait had explained.

"Oh, sure," he muttered, slapping at his ear.

The outside landscaping lights shone brightly enough to see by. Bill untied the netting on one side. When the gauzy folds dropped forward to enfold him, he felt like a caterpillar, all curled up in a cocoon, ready to sleep.

Later, when he woke up, the room was pitch-dark. It took him a few seconds to remember Aunt Cait's saying that the outside lights went off automatically at three in the morning.

As his eyes gradually adjusted to the dark, the white gauzy cloth looked so much like hovering ghosts, Bill wanted to scream.

It took every single bit of his willpower to take hold of the netting, bunch it up, and tie it back by the headboard. With the side of his bed closest to the window open again, Bill felt better. He only hoped he'd be able to fall back to sleep fast. If he had to lie awake in this strange ghost-filled room, he might just start thinking too much about Mom.

The trouble was, Bill had the awful feeling Mom wasn't bothering to think about *him*. Dad either. What they both liked thinking about was the food business.

Long before this summer had even started, Bill remembered hearing their excited voices planning and plotting their Special Joint Venture, which would keep them Very Busy all over Eastern Europe and Scandinavia for eight whole weeks.

All his parents' conversations during mealtimes and weekends had to do with something they called the new global market.

Well, he hated that new global market and—

Bill felt hot tears welling up in his eyes. He punched his pillow with all his strength. "I hate them too," he whispered.

Two seconds later he heard it, right outside the window. His entire body went stiff.

The noise came again, louder this time.

Someone—a homicidal maniac probably, with a very bad cough—was standing right outside his window!

Bill strained his eyes to see beyond the glass. All he really wanted to do was bury his head under the pillow. Instead he turned his head away from the window.

What was on the porch?

If only he could shut his eyes and wait awhile, maybe he'd wake up and realize this was only a bad dream.

But he didn't dare close his eyes, and he knew he wasn't dreaming.

To keep himself from yelling, Bill tried counting under his breath. "One-one hundred, two-one hundred, three-one hundred, four—"

An eerie sense that he was being watched made him stop counting and swivel his head around to stare through the window into the darkness. He gasped.

Two fiery-yellow stones with brilliant green centers, each stone the shape and size of a boiled egg, were staring back at him like . . . *eyes!*

Bill quit breathing.

Strange snickering noises were followed by another bout of loud coughing. As he listened and watched, and gradually started breathing again, the big yellow gemstones blinked on and off a few times.

They got smaller and smaller, their glowing green centers becoming pinpoints of light. Then he couldn't see the twin lights at all. Cautiously sitting up in bed, Bill thought he heard muffled footsteps moving away, around the porch toward the front steps.

Listening as hard as he could, Bill heard the soft *thud-thud* of feet stepping down—down—down.

He wondered how it could be that he was frozen solid and dripping sweat at the same time. He wondered, too, how he could be so sure about those eyes.

And he *was* sure. He just knew. They were panther eyes!

No one, Bill decided, not Aunt Cait, not all the experts in Florida, could tell him it wasn't true. There'd been a real live panther roaming free on the porch right outside his window. A big one too.

These subtropics are horrible, he thought. What next?

2.

Muck, Rot, and Stinky Annie Stokes

"Burial mound? You mean we're sifting dead Calusas? Bones and toenails and stuff?"

The dig site was midway up the shell mound. Standing opposite Annie Stokes at the sifter screen, Bill glanced over his shoulder. Below it was sunny, the beach sand white and the water like tinted blue glass. Up here, surrounded by bushes and scrawny scrub pines, it was cool, the seabreeze riffling through the leaves and pine needles.

It looked peaceful but . . . "Hey, Annie, maybe we shouldn't mess with Calusas' special old bones."

In the movies dead Native Americans always got upset when people disturbed their sacred graves.

"We're not messing, and we're not digging for treasure either," she said. "Archaeology is like detective work, that's what my dad says. We search for clues to unsolved mysteries of the past."

"What unsolved mysteries?"

"If you stop goofing and start shaking your side of the screen, I'll tell you one."

"I *am* shaking," he said. "You're the one who's goofing."

"So maybe I won't tell you a mystery. Maybe it's humanly impossible to talk and shake at the same time."

"That's what *you* think," he wanted to say.

"Okay," she said, "only because you should know what to look for. Not because I like to talk or anything."

"Oh, no, nothing like that."

"The Calusas' ancestors may have lived around here for nearly six thousand years. We're only starting to learn about them, so *they're* the mystery. All over these islands the Calusas built sacred burial mounds from seashells and—"

"I know," he said, "Aunt Cait already told me."

Annie gave him a dirty look. "Did she tell you that after they got to be super-powerful and filthy rich, lots of Calusas disappeared practically overnight? *Poof!* They vanished like smoke.

"*Smoke.* That's a clue, Billy."

"It *is?*"

But Annie didn't give him time to think about it.

"King Calos is my favorite," she said. "He lived over four hundred years ago. Know what? *I* think he's watching us while we work. What I think is, he wants us to know what happened. I told my dad that, and he said he sometimes gets that feeling too. He said Horr's Island has Calusa spirit!"

"Really?" Bill glanced over his shoulder again. "Who's this King Calos?"

"He was a great Calusa chief, only they called him Cacique, or King. Anyway, he was so smart, he formed a federation. Because he was so powerful, all the other Florida tribes joined the federation. They had to bring him food and great gifts all the time.

"The Calusas were tall," she continued. "King Calos was over seven feet tall. And on special occasions he wore a three-foot-high feathered turban which made him *ten* feet tall."

"This king guy," Bill asked, "he's watching us? How? If he lived over four hundred years ago, what's he use for eyes?"

"Spirit eyes," Annie said in her know-it-all voice. "A few centuries is nothing for a powerful spirit like King Calos. I read that he communed with his dead ancestors while he was alive. You know, like psychics do? So why wouldn't he be able to commune even better now that he's dead and *we're* alive?

"Sure," she said in a dreamy voice, "an incredible alpha man like him can probably do anything."

Annie Stokes was the incredible one, Bill thought, a regular junior *Jeopardy!*-champ type kid. One thing he'd liked about her right off was she was exactly his size. What he didn't like was finding out she was a year younger and his size.

When he and Aunt Cait had arrived at Horr's Island this morning, Annie had been waiting with three university students on the beach.

Since summer was off-season, every excavation but one was sealed until October. "We'll concentrate our efforts on a single pit," Aunt Cait had explained, "so consider yourself part of my summer skeleton crew, Billy."

A skeleton crew on a burial mound made sense, but he didn't have to like it, did he?

"Hey, Annie," Bill asked, "is that old bones I smell? Whew, it stinks up here."

He'd noticed the too-sweet smell after they'd left the beach and climbed halfway up the mound to the roped-off open pit.

"Old bones don't stink, Billy, but post rot and mangrove muck and tannin do. Today, though, the stink is mostly me."

He stared after her as she left her place at the sifter screen and walked away. He watched her as she rummaged through her blue backpack hanging from a tree branch.

"Come over here, Billy, and take a good hard whiff. Tell me what you think. I need your honest opinion."

She had her head down, her hair hiding her eyes as she unscrewed the cap from a small white bottle.

Curious, Bill walked over and took the bottle she held out.

"Go on," Annie urged, "take a nice big sniff."

He sniffed. "Man, what's that?" he gasped, handing the bottle back.

In his entire lifetime Bill had never smelled anything as bad as that. His breath backtracked up his nostrils so fast, he felt a piercing pain in his brain.

"Get that cap back on. What is it, anyway, thousand-year-old throw-up?"

"Essence of fish. I caught a mullet and boiled it down to oil and bones. I strained out the oil and added secret herbs and spices. It's been marinating a month and a half, aged to perfection.

"See, what I'm trying to do is replicate the ancient Calusa formula for insect repellent. We really need it in this line of work."

Replicate? With every second he knew her Annie got worse. She was a living example of what could happen to a kid who hung around archaeologists too much.

"We could do a trial test with the formula today. If it does the job, we could cook up a big batch for everyone to use. Open your hand."

He backed away. "You think I'm putting that stuff on me?"

"Why not? Mosquitoes here get vicious. You'd rather smell than itch, wouldn't you?"

When he shook his head, Annie shrugged and dabbed the oil behind her ears, on the insides of her wrists, even on her face.

"You'll be sorry," she told him.

And Bill was. Working the sifter screen with a girl who smelled like rotted fish wasn't his idea of a good time.

For several minutes they shook the screen in silence. Whenever the soil fell through the screen, they sorted through the debris left on top.

Every bit of broken shell, pottery, and bird and fish bone had to be studied, sorted, and put into clear bags or on the proper tray. Annie had to write and make diagrams in a field notebook about everything they found. It took so much time!

"Wouldn't it be great if we found something good today?" Annie asked. "What I dream about is being on the scene when something important happens. Not too long ago, off the south tip of Marco, guess what they found?"

"What?" he muttered, trying not to breathe.

"A twenty-five-hundred-year-old skeleton. It must have been *so* neat to reach out and touch someone from five hundred B.C.!"

"Really?" He couldn't think what else to say.

From time to time he stole glances at Annie as she worked. He still couldn't figure out whether she had a suntan or her face was one solid freckle. Her hair was wild-curly, darkish blonde and long. Most of her curls were held back from her face by a rubber band.

Annie caught him looking. She reached behind her neck, ripped off the rubber band, and shook out her hair until it hung like a curtain in front of her face.

"Don't you wish *you* had this emergency mosquito net handy? Calusas had long hair. They could do this, too, in a pinch. Too bad you can't, with your hair so short and all. I'm telling you, this oil is just what you need."

"Ouch!" But the sting of his first mosquito bite didn't change his mind. Nothing would make him put that gross stuff on his skin. "Knock it off," he said.

She did. Instead, Annie told him all kinds of personal stuff. Her parents were divorced, she said, but three months ago her mother had gotten married again, to a Frenchman.

Annie said archaeology was in her blood. Her father was an Egyptologist, and until he died last year her grandfather had been one too. "I'm more of a naturalist," she explained. "I'm going to be an environmental archaeologist."

Before he could ask her what that was, Annie changed the subject. "Seen any pictures of the Key Marco Cat-god?"

"My aunt has a big poster of it."

"Don't you think the Marco cat statue looks a lot like the Egyptian Cat-goddess, Bastet?"

"Who?"

"She was a sun-goddess in the form of a cat. Lots of civilizations worshiped cats. And if you look at the map of Florida, it's the shape of a cat's paw."

Bill guessed he would check a map later, but about one thing he'd already made up his mind. The Key Marco Cat-god was a *guy* god, not a goddess. Aunt Cait had said "as you choose," hadn't she?

Annie walked back over to the tree, opened the big cooler, and poured pineapple juice into paper cups. She came back and handed him one.

"Syl-via would die if she caught me doing this without washing my hands first. Sylvia's my grandmother, and she's a super-fastidious person."

Annie took a big gulp of juice. "She hates digs because digs mean dirt. Since Grandpa's been gone, she complains a lot. It's probably because she doesn't have interesting, fun stuff to do."

She pointed to the other workers. "Look over there. Your aunt looks good, doesn't she? That's because she does have interesting stuff to do. She looks like an Indiana Jones woman."

Annie was right. In her purple pith helmet, khaki pants, and safari-type shirt and boots, Aunt Cait did sort of look like an explorer in a jungle movie.

"Hey, Billy, hold still. Don't move for a second."

In a flash Annie had dumped out the rest of her juice and was beside him, scooping something off the back of his shirt with her cup. "There," she said. "Gotcha!"

Frozen in place, Bill watched as she calmly carried the cup to a bush and deposited the contents into the leaves. He glimpsed something small and shiny yellow with legs scurrying out of sight.

"What was that?" he gasped.

"A scorpion. Not very big, though."

Bill glared at her. "What did you let it go for? It'll just come back."

Annie gave him a funny look. "What did you want me to do?"

"Kill it! Smash it! Scorpions sting to death, don't they? It could've *killed* me!"

"It's not deadly, Billy. And, anyway, it lives here. Scorpions try to stay out of our way, so we do the same. To keep out of trouble, we keep our eyes wide open."

Bill groaned. Instead of wearing long-sleeved shirts and long pants, maybe he should wear a space suit.

"Relax, Billy," Annie said, "it's almost lunchtime."

Relax? No chance of that on Horr's Island, where scorpions had the right-of-way and a too-smart-for-her-age girl walked around stinking up the place worse than it already smelled.

If this king of the Calusas *was* hanging around watching them like a hawk, Bill bet, by now Annie's smell had blown him away.

And Annie thought he was looking forward to lunch?

3.

Disaster on the Dock

So much sky! It was like a giant blue tent pegged down at the edges by palm trees. Bill still couldn't get over how much more sky there was off the west coast of Florida than in New Jersey.

The sun blazed, huge and bright and hot. At three in the afternoon they'd left Horr's Island and his first day at the dig was done. They were on their way back to Marco Island, to the Riverside Club, the apartment complex where Annie lived. She'd invited them to stop on the way home for a swim in the club pool.

Aunt Cait steered her boat, the *Island Lady*, over the glittering blue waters. Cool breezes whacked at him, whipping away the worst of his sweat. Bracing himself on the seat, Bill tipped his head back and opened his mouth wide. If he gulped in enough fresh air, maybe the fish-rot taste in his mouth would go away.

"Bill, look!"

A dolphin broke water, leaping high and half-twisting in midair before slipping back under.

A Flipper, sleek and silvery, exactly like the TV ads for Sea World, and so close! The dolphin was the best thing he'd seen since he'd started this vacation. It kept up with the boat, doing all kinds of gymnastics, just for them.

Past the No Wake signs Aunt Cait slowed the boat's motor to a quiet hum. A bunch of fat-bottomed brown pelicans with beaks like pocketbooks were lined up along the dock. Three more pelicans were perched atop poles, and those three were giving him the evil eye.

Maybe that bad-looking pelican patrol wasn't planning to let him on their dock. It could be they didn't even want him taking a swim in their pool this afternoon.

Actually the pelicans reminded him a lot of some kids in school—his worst enemies: Cory Barrister and Rob Lewis and Stillman Kobe. This past year, whenever he'd had to walk past Cory and his friends, Bill had played Invisible Kid so they wouldn't see him and call him "runt" or "shorty."

Okay, so he'd be Invisible Kid for the pelicans too. Maybe they'd look right through him when Aunt Cait brought her boat in to the dock. He hoped so; he really didn't like the looks of those big birds.

"Over here!"

It was Annie, standing on the dock, waving at him like crazy.

He glanced away fast.

Aunt Cait cruised the *Island Lady* slowly toward the dock. Watching her parallel-park her boat beside a much larger one, Bill half-closed his eyes, imagining himself doing the boat parking and—

"Over here!" Annie shouted again.

He opened his eyes and craned his neck just in time to see Annie—barefoot—racing toward him along this dock, waving the bottle of bug juice.

Annie shook the bottle back and forth. She grinned and pretended to pour it out, pretended to—

Man! She was waiting to get him with the stuff!

Aunt Cait jumped up onto the dock first, and the pelicans moved back. While she wrapped the boat line several times around a bollard and secured it with a thick knot, Bill planned how best to jump up onto the dock in a single move.

But before he had time to worry about it, Aunt Cait reached down to him. He grabbed her hand and she yanked him up, no problem.

"Next time," she said, "maybe you'll tie up for me. I'll teach you the knots." He caught Aunt Cait's quick wink.

"Remember, I'm not as young as I used to be." She lifted her pith helmet. "Don't believe me? See? Gray hair."

Bill laughed. "Gray *and* brown, Aunt Cait," he said, "like pelican feathers."

"Why, you're right," she said, smiling.

"Hi, Dr. Tucker, hi, Billy," Annie said behind him.

He turned to see her smiling like a happy cat, one hand hidden behind her back.

Aunt Cait jumped back into her boat. "You two go ahead," she said. "I forgot the sun block. I'll meet you poolside in a few minutes."

Annie didn't move.

"Better not," Bill said.

"Well, you wouldn't try it voluntarily." She had the cap off the bug-oil bottle and was tipping it toward him.

Over her shoulder Billy saw someone else headed their way. The tall, thin lady in the blinding-white dress didn't exactly have gray hair. It was silver, so smooth and perfect it looked as if she'd taped aluminum foil to her head.

The silver-headed lady struggled along the dock toward them, her high heels catching, every few steps, between the boards. Her lips and eyes grew narrower as she came closer. Everything about her looked skinny and silvery, sharp and straight—a needle woman!

Bill knew just who she was—Sylvia. Sylvia, Annie's fastidious grandmother, the one who didn't have much fun. He could see why; who could laugh with such squinchy lips and slitty eyes?

"Oh, so you don't believe I'll do it, huh?" Annie said in a spoiled-brat voice.

Bill relaxed. He was safe from Annie now that her grandmother'd showed up. He shrugged to let her know he wasn't worried.

Needle Woman was almost right behind Annie, and she had a hairbrush in her hand.

Should he warn Annie? For her own good? "Hey, Annie," he whispered.

But it was too late for warnings.

Annie's eyes went wide with shock as the bristles of the hairbrush grabbed at her tangled curls. "Ouch," she yelled, "stop!"

Just in time Bill stepped back, nudging aside two of the pelicans. The bottle flew from Annie's fingers.

Up—up—and over her shoulder the juice flew and then came down again, splashing everywhere—

"What in heaven's name? Vivianne, what *is* this repulsive, disgusting— *Vivianne!*"

Needle Woman could really yell, Bill thought, taking three more fast steps backward.

"Grandma—oh, my gosh, Grandma, I'm *so* sorry!"

"What is this? Tell me—argh, argh—*this minute!* Argh—*look at me!"*

The stink was bad enough to gag a grandmother, all right, bad enough to knock her eyes wide open too. Silver-gray eyes. It figured.

Annie stood there with her head bent, staring down at her bare toes. Bill couldn't see her eyes with all her front curls hanging down, but he could hear little noises coming from under there. Was she crying?

No, she was whispering to him. As Needle Woman spit into a balled-up tissue and used it to rub frantically at her dress front, Bill heard Annie's whisper blowing through her curls.

"Don't ever, *ever* call me Vivianne, Billy, hear me? I'm *not* Vivianne, I'm Annie. Just plain Annie."

She *was* crying, her teardrops plopping on the dock and on her sun-browned feet.

"Vivianne, come here!"

Bill couldn't back away another step. Already the heels of his hightops were about an inch from the edge of the dock.

One great thing, though, the pelicans weren't hanging out by him anymore. They were much more interested in Annie's grandmother's fishiness, crowding around her high heels, fighting each other for the best position.

"Oh, my gosh, Bill," Annie whispered, "now I've really done it."

"Ah, don't worry ," he whispered back. "She'll probably only—I don't know—get over it?"

Aunt Cait was back on the dock, hurrying toward them, a concerned expression on her face. "What on earth is going on?" she asked. "What happened? Sylvia, are you all right?"

"Nothing is all right, Cait. How can you even ask that? Smell me—just smell me! What is this ghastly substance?"

One look at his aunt's face and Bill knew she was struggling not to laugh. He sure hoped she wouldn't. He hated to think what would happen if she did.

Already Needle Woman was hopping up and down, she was so mad.

Or it could be she was hopping up and down because of the pelicans pecking at her ankles.

At last Annie's grandmother turned and hurried back along the dock, with the pelican patrol waddling right after her.

"We'll swim another day, Bill," Aunt Cait said.

Before he could answer she put her arm around Annie. "Want to tell me what happened?"

Bill had to hand it to Annie. She did the explaining and didn't try blaming it even a little bit on him.

Aunt Cait listened and gave Annie a hug and a few pats on the back, and it seemed to help. At least Annie wasn't shedding tears on her bare toes anymore.

She was actually staring straight at him. Bill didn't think he liked the fierce look in her eyes very much.

"Remember, Billy, don't call me anything except Annie. Annie Stokes, that's who I am!"

"Okay, Annie," he said, "and I'm *Bill*. Just plain Bill. Don't call me Billy anymore."

"Deal," she said, and they shook on it. She turned and walked away, her small feet stomping hard on the weathered boards.

He watched her until she disappeared around a corner past the pool area. The pool looked good. Bill wished things had worked out differently and they didn't have to wait for another day to swim.

"Come to think of it," Aunt Cait said, "I've been calling you both Bill and Billy. Confusing. Bill *is* much better. It suits you."

4.

Soft Evidence

From the Riverside Club to Aunt Cait's dock wasn't far. What took time was her having to steer the *Island Lady* slowly through the narrow back canals toward home. Part of the trip she didn't talk. Part of it she did. She told him a story she'd heard about a vacationer.

"So, there she was, Bill," Aunt Cait said, "a first-time visitor to Marco Island, walking along the boulevard early one summer day. She was on her way to buy the morning newspaper.

"She strolled along, obviously with no idea of what was close behind her, *chasing* her along the sidewalk. It chased her right up to the front door of the 7-Eleven."

"What was it?" he asked.

"It wasn't until she was safely inside the store that she—and everyone else inside—heard the scratching on the glass door. Only then did she realize what a close call she'd had. It was an *alligator*."

Aunt Cait shook her head. "Poor woman, that ruined her vacation, I'm sure. Poor alligator too. With its natural habitat taken away, it probably didn't know if it was coming or going."

"Maybe it only wanted Gatorade, Aunt Cait," Bill said, "or a Slurpee."

Not that he thought the close-call convenience store story was so funny. Bill figured he had had enough wild things to worry about across Aunt Cait's road and at the dig. Now he'd have to worry about people-chasing alligators.

Alligators couldn't climb porch steps, could they?

"What color eyes do alligators have?" he asked.

So far he hadn't told her about his panther. *Maybe I will*, he thought, *and maybe I won't*.

"Daytime eyes? I'd say muddy-yellow, if there *is* such a color. At night, with a flashlight aimed right, alligator eyes are fire-engine red."

"Do they make any . . . noises?"

"They do indeed," Aunt Cait said. "They *bellow*."

Behind his sunglasses he blinked. He didn't want to hear anymore.

What would Mom say if she could see him now? For a few seconds he put himself in his mother's shoes. He could just see her, standing over there on the grassy bank of the canal. Because of the blazing sunlight she had to shade her eyes to see him clearly.

Watching him and Aunt Cait cruising through the

quiet blue-green waters, heading home, Mom was impressed. She thought he looked great in his new cap and cool shades, and—right at that second—she discovered how much she missed him.

In fact, she was actually crying because of how much she missed him. She wished she wasn't so far away in Europe.

"How about helping me tie up?"

The color of the water changed as they neared Aunt Cait's dock. This water wasn't greenish-blue, it was muddy-yellow, like alligators' daytime eyes.

"I don't know the knot yet," he told her.

"True," Aunt Cait said. "For now, then, reach out and grab hold of the post when we get closer. That part you can do, right?"

"Right."

Grabbing the post with both hands, Bill felt the pull on his biceps. He guessed if he could work out like this twice a day, his muscles would be hard as moon rocks by the end of the summer. Aunt Cait was right; he *could* do this part.

"Thanks," Aunt Cait said.

"You're welcome," he answered, rushing past her to climb the back steps to the second-storey porch. It felt excellent having his hightops off the ground for the day. Even better was stepping inside the cool, dim stillness of the house and hearing the door close.

Before he headed down the hall to his room, Bill paused in the doorway to the living room. "Hey, dudes," he whispered to the masks, "I'm *baaack*."

A short time later, after a great shower, he padded barefoot along his hall past Aunt Cait's study to the screened section of the porch she called the lanai.

She was writing in her field notebook, but she glanced up and gave him a smile. "Help yourself," she murmured, gesturing with her pen.

A pitcher of iced tea on a wicker tray waited beneath the big green leaves of a potted plant. Bill poured himself a glassful, sat down, and rested his head against the cushy back of the lounger. *Ah*, he thought, *this is the life*. He was sure his father would say exactly that if he were here.

Another thing Bill was sure of: he was hungry. Breakfast had been hours ago, one fried-egg sandwich, which he'd gulped down on the way to Horr's Island this morning. And if he counted no lunch at all, Bill thought it was no wonder he was starving to death.

Cook!

Sometimes it worked with Mom when he sent her a direct message from his mind. If he repeated the message a lot, Mom or Dad would usually pick up his mind hint and get busy making food. They'd think it was their own idea.

Cook, Aunt Cait, cook!

"Well, now, Bill, how about some supper? Don't know about you, but my stomach's growling at me."

He laughed. "Mine's roaring."

Bill was starved for television too. So far, he hadn't been able to find Aunt Cait's set. Yesterday, after he'd worked up the nerve to ask, all she'd said was, "Oh, sure, it's around here somewhere."

What kind of answer was that? Did she have a television set or not? If he'd known this was going to happen, he could've brought along his own TV, VCR, and all his favorite videos.

Man, he thought, *if I have to sit and watch Aunt Cait read and write every night this summer, I'll go totally nutso.*

No matter how he hated doing it, Bill knew he'd have to ask again. He would beg her: "Please, Aunt Cait, find your TV!"

After supper, though, he decided not to mention it. If it was around somewhere, he'd find it.

For something else to do Bill wandered out onto the porch. He jogged back and forth a few times, working off his food. Anyway, that's what he wanted Aunt Cait to think. What he was really doing was spying. On himself.

The sun had set, but the landscaping lights weren't on yet, so the porch was dark and shadowy. Crouched outside his bedroom window, Bill flattened his nose against the glass. He couldn't see a thing.

That meant the panther couldn't've seen even a piece of him. Disappointed, he got to his feet. Did the panther's not seeing him through the window mean it would never visit again?

Wait a minute! Cats could see in the dark, couldn't they? He'd find out. He could casually ask Aunt Cait for a book about the Florida panther. She'd probably be thrilled that he was showing an interest.

If only he could find proof now, some good hard evidence that the panther had really been here in the middle of the night.

Backing up, Bill leaned against the porch rail to think about it.

That's when he felt it. Something fluffy-soft against the palm of his left hand. It felt like—*fur*.

A teensy tuft of fur maybe, but, wow, if the panther had rubbed up against this porch rail, or stood up on its hind legs for a second, well—

Carefully he pulled away the bit of panther fur from the crack in the wood. With the proof in his hand, Bill raced back to the lanai, yanked open the screen door, and glanced around.

Good! Aunt Cait was still upstairs taking her shower. Now he'd have privacy inspecting his evidence. If the fur was tawny-yellow, it would be panther proof.

Close to the lamplight, Bill slowly spread out his fingers and looked. It *was* brownish-yellow.

Except, when he stroked the tiny piece of fluff, he felt a hard spine smack in the middle. Not panther fur. Not hard evidence. Just a dumb feather from some dumb bird hanging out on Aunt Cait's porch.

It wasn't until after he was in bed with the light turned out that he remembered something that helped make his disappointed feeling go away. If Aunt Cait was right, then finding the little feather wasn't so bad. It might even be a good omen, a *messenger* feather.

5.

A Few Great Gifts

"Wake up, Bill, jump into your bathing suit, grab a towel. You don't want to miss it."

He opened his eyes and yawned. It wasn't even light yet.

"Coming, Aunt Cait," he said.

Still half-asleep, he put on his bathing suit, pulled a sweatshirt over his head, and took off running, trailing a large towel behind him.

Aunt Cait was already on the front porch.

"Miss what?" he asked.

She smiled. "Wait and see. Come on, let's go."

Walking medium fast on the deserted road, it took them about ten minutes to reach Tigertail Beach. It turned out to be a great beach, with little wooden walkways and bridges spanning the sand dunes, and lots of tall yellow grass waving backward in the cool breeze.

"Is that wheat?"

"Close," she answered. "Sea oats. Important too; roots anchor the sand, keep the beach from blowing away."

He nodded, surprised to see so many people at the beach so early. And all of them, old ones and young ones, even the littlest kids, were bent over as they walked near the frothy edge of the water.

After Bill helped Aunt Cait spread the striped blanket on the sand, he looked again. The people were still doing it, all doubled over, shuffling along the shoreline.

"What're they doing?" he whispered.

"They're shelling," Aunt Cait said. "First tide carries in lots of lovely specimens, piles them up in rows. Before sunrise is always the best time. Word's gotten around: Tigertail Beach is a sheller's paradise."

She pointed across the water. "See that little sandbar out there, Bill? That's where we'll go. That's where the real treasures can be found."

"Treasures?" Treasures might be worth getting up early for, he thought. "You mean, gold and stuff?"

Aunt Cait laughed as she set her lumpy leopard-print backpack on the beach blanket. "Shell treasures. You'd be surprised how valuable certain shells are."

"Oh."

"Let's start," she said. "Most of the way over the water is shallow, so we can walk. There's only a short stretch of deeper water where we'll have to swim. You *did* say you knew how to swim?"

"Sure," he muttered. What did she think, a kid with

a pool in his own backyard wouldn't know how to swim? Last summer and the first part of this summer, he'd put in a lot of practice time.

"Good," she said. "If you're lucky, maybe you'll find that first special shell for your summer collection."

"What summer collection?"

"Why, whatever you find and like and choose to keep." She shrugged. "I don't know, it's entirely up to you."

"Okay," he said doubtfully, plopping down on the edge of the blanket to take off his hightops.

"I should warn you," she said. "Out farther the bottom gets mucky. Be careful, don't step on anything sharp."

Sharp? He swallowed hard. Like what, Jaws?

But Aunt Cait was already heading straight across the white-powder sand to the water. He watched her as she waded in. In her purple flowered bathing suit, she reminded him of a tattooed lady.

"Hate your happy guts, Aunt Cait," he whispered as he ran across the sand.

"Water's great," he yelled, wading toward her. He hoped he sounded like a regular, rowdy kid at the beach.

"Isn't it?" Aunt Cait's eyes matched the water, he noticed. "I love the beach first thing in the morning, don't you?"

"Sure," he said.

Wading across wasn't bad until, without warning, Aunt Cait began acting crazy, flippering around in the water beside him. *Aunt Cait was pretending to be a dolphin!*

First she'd dive underwater and disappear for a few seconds, then she'd surface with a major splash. She rolled over and over, her arms pressed to her sides, her hands and feet jutting out at right angles.

Worst of all she made noises, her tongue hitting the roof of her mouth. *"Click-click. Click-click-click."*

Bill couldn't believe it. He tried not looking at her, but he thought he'd probably better keep one eye on her.

Aunt Cait's next triple roll brought her right beside him.

"Click-click-click in Dolphinese means 'Wanna ride?' Dolphins do that, take turns towing each other," she told him, "especially dolphin mothers with their kids."

The water was only up past Aunt Cait's ribs, but it was already licking Bill's chin. He began to swim.

"Click-click-click! Hop on, Bill, take a breather."

Hop on? He tried swimming faster to get away from her. No way was he going to let her play dolphin mother with *him.*

But his breath was coming in hard gasps. His shoulder blades were killing him, and his legs were—what was that?

Underwater—around his legs—*something!*

Panicked, Bill thrashed his arms and legs. He fought to keep his head above water. He went under and came up again, gasping and blinking. The salt water stung his eyes so bad he couldn't see.

All at once he felt Aunt Cait's solid presence beside him, felt her arm, strong and firm, around his waist, felt himself lifted and turned.

Before he knew it, he was out of the water, lying crossways on her back, only his ribs touching her as she swam smoothly forward.

With his head craned and his arms and legs flung out, he guessed if the shell stoopers were looking, they'd think he was a sea turtle, not a dolphin's hitch-hiking kid. It was great getting his breath back, resting, not getting his legs jawed off.

"Angelfish," Aunt Cait said. "Look down. School's letting out."

Bill looked in time to see small white fish rushing by. He guessed it had been the brush of angelfish fins against his legs he'd felt, not a shark or a barracuda.

The water was so clear, he could see to the sandy bottom. It wasn't blue-green water though, it was pink.

"Turn around and look," she said again as he slid off her back. "Stand up while you're at it, the water's shallow here."

Standing there, with his back to the sandbar, Bill shaded his eyes with his hands against the glare. He watched everything around him turn neon pink as the biggest fireball sun he'd ever seen rolled slowly uphill in the sky above the tallest palm trees and high-rise condos.

"Wow," he whispered.

One after another new colors turned the calm water around him to pink-purple, purple-red, red-orange, copper-penny orange, the copper pennies turning into solid gold. Sky, water, sand, even his own skin looked like spilled pirate's treasure.

Aunt Cait was right. If they hadn't hurried, he would've missed it. He could see for himself; once the sun started rising, it wouldn't wait for anyone.

It's not Sunday, Bill thought, *it's Sun Day*.

Aunt Cait, a few feet away, was bent over, reaching for something in the wet sand. Hey, if he didn't get busy, she'd probably beat him to it, find the best shell on the bar.

"Ouch!" Bill saw a little golden horn wedged between his toes.

Aunt Cait walked toward him. "What's that?" he asked, pointing at his toes.

"Oh, aren't you the lucky one," she said. "I think you've found yourself a rare yellow conch. Let's take a closer look."

When he had the shell in his hand, she bent to study it.

"What did you call it, Aunt Cait?"

"Conch . . . spelled with a *ch* but pronounced 'konk.' The species isn't rare, but the color is. Such a lovely lemon-sauce yellow."

"It's not the sun making it that color?"

"No, Bill, I'm almost positive you've found yourself a treasure. Sitting on one of those empty shelves in your room, this little shell will shine with importance.

"Let's sit for a while," she said. "You admire your treasure, and I'll say my thank you notes."

"Thank you notes? What for?"

"For the day," she said quietly, "for the perfect shell you found, for you, for my own good fortune—for my good health and for the gift of being able to do what I love to do and be where I love to be."

Aunt Cait's eyes were closed as she spoke. He took a close-up look at her wrinkles. To him it looked as if someone had pressed a spiderweb to her skin and left it there permanently. If she'd keep her eyes shut awhile longer, he could probably count the web lines.

"For the old reliable Great Spirit sun, I'm thankful too."

"You are?"

"Think how long it's been going on. Sunrise is time-less! Think of the Calusas standing here, where we are, watching the new day begin. Think of those ancients who came *before* them. Imagine, your own great-grandson might stand here one summer morning in years to come, watching the sun rise, wondering about his ancient ancestor, Bill Carven."

"Me—ancient?" He laughed.

Her eyes fluttered but didn't open. "For me being present at sunrise is like attending a church service. Do you see what I mean?"

"I guess so." He squinted at the golden water. "That's who the Great Spirit is—the sun?"

"Everything and everyone is part of the Great Spirit. You, me, the sun, this warm sand, the Gulf breeze blowing on our faces. All the creatures in nature, those with fur, fins, wings, four legs, two legs, tails, roots, branches, and petals. The list is endless because the Great Spirit is endless."

Aunt Cait opened her eyes, but she gazed straight ahead, not at him. "The sun's a magnificent visible symbol of the circle we call Life."

Bill didn't know what to say. Not that he had to say anything. The faraway expression on her face made him think she'd forgotten he was even there.

When Aunt Cait spoke again, she surprised him. "About your shell. Did you know it's a skeleton?"

A skeleton? He stared at the shell.

"Your skeleton's inside, and your body—tissue, muscle, and the rest—grow on and around it. For a mollusk it's the other way around. Its body grows *inside* its skeleton. And when the mollusk wants to move on, it leaves its bones on the beach for us to find and admire.

"If I'm right, Bill, what you have is a dwarf queen conch, but ask Grant. I'm not the shell expert, he is. He should be back from the Glades today. I left a message on his answering machine, invited him to have dinner with us.

"Wait until you meet him, Bill." She smiled. "Grant will spin you tales you won't believe."

He laughed. "That's nothing. I spin *myself* tales I can't believe."

"We'll have to do grocery shopping this afternoon," she said. "On our way over to Publix, we'll stop at the art league. I've thought of a gift I want you to have for your summer collection."

He lay on his stomach, letting the sun fire laser

beams at his back while Aunt Cait wandered the sand-bar, chatting with long-legged wading birds. Bill reached out to touch the crown of his queen conch shell. A gift for him? What could it be?

Really my third gift today, he thought dreamily, *if I count this shell and the Great Spirit sunrise.*

6 ∎

No Fangs

The Art League of Marco Island reminded him of Aunt Cait's living room. Walking into the cool gallery with its soaring-high ceiling and paintings stuck all over the walls, he felt about two inches tall.

Everywhere he looked, eyes looked back: slitty gators' eyes, beady birds' eyes, even peacocks' feather-eyes.

But if it was hard having so many paintings give him the once-over, that was nothing next to the way the gallery lady was studying him from the top of his head to his hightops.

"So this is your great-nephew, Cait. Bill, isn't it? How do you like Marco, Bill?"

Her name was Maggie Brunaldi, and she was so junked up with shell necklaces and bracelets, she clattered as she talked.

"S'okay," he mumbled.

"*Okay?* Cait, I thought you said—"

"Bill's still getting used to our island, but he is excited about seeing what we have for him today. I though he might like looking around the gallery too. Maggie, you *do* remember what we talked about on the phone?"

He saw them giving each other high eyebrows and hand signals.

"Why don't we head for the gift shop," Maggie said, "and not keep Bill in suspense a moment longer."

The sooner everyone stopped looking at him, the better, he decided. That Calusa man in the bigger-than-life painting over there especially. The giant Calusa's feather-plumed hat took up the whole top third of the picture, and he even had Maggie beat when it came to shell jewels.

"Hey, wait!" The soles of his hightops made a horrible squeak as he stopped short on the polished floor tiles. "Is that King Calos?"

Something about his bark-colored face, his bulging tattooed muscles, and, especially, the towering headdress seemed familiar.

Maggie beamed at him. "However did you know? You've been here how long?"

"How *did* you know?" Aunt Cait asked.

"Annie," Bill said, studying the feather turban.

It would take a whole summer's worth of feather hunting to make one of those.

"King Calos is right. I do prefer *Calos* over *Carlos*,"

Maggie said. "Never mind that the Spanish explorers thought they were flattering him by calling him after their king. What I think, Bill, is that King Calos only pretended to change his name as a gesture of good faith and friendship."

"You know, I tend to agree with you, Maggie, but do you think we could—"

"Oh, don't mind me, Cait. I promise not to get all wound up on the subject today. It's only that talking with you reminds me."

Bill couldn't imagine this tall, great-looking Calusa king giving up his true name, not for anyone.

"The painting was done by a fine local artist, a most commanding presence in this gallery, I must say."

Aunt Cait smiled. "Maggie, lead the way, *please.*"

Following them across the quiet gallery, Bill felt the king's dark-eyed gaze boring holes between his shoulder blades. What must it be like, he wondered, to be so strong and tall and important that you stayed that way, even in a picture?

Maybe that's what Annie'd meant when she'd talked about King Calos's powerful spirit—how he could do anything.

The gift shop was tiny. Maggie told him all about the art league's plans to make the place bigger and better. He listened, but he was glad when Aunt Cait interrupted.

"Could you show it to him, please, Mag?"

While Maggie messed around behind the counter, opening drawers, rustling tissue paper, and breathing hard, Bill paced around, looking at all kinds of fascinating stuff on the shelves and in glass cases.

He should've known Aunt Cait would make him come here. Next to the dig site and her own house, this was probably her third-favorite place on Marco Island.

"Here we are," Maggie announced, "only we might have a problem. It just so happens today you have a choice. One is ceramic, one is carved from cypress wood."

Aunt Cait waved Maggie's suggestion away. "There is *not* a choice," she said. "Bill wants it to be as close to the real thing as he can get it. The original was carved from cypress, so cypress is what he wants."

I do? "That's right," he murmured, secretly glad someone knew what they were talking about.

"Settled!" Maggie exclaimed. Shell bracelets racketing, she carefully removed layers of tissue paper as if they were mummy wrappings. At last she held up a small reddish-brown object for his inspection.

It was the Key Marco Cat-god!

"Like it, Bill?"

"Yes," he said. "Thanks, Aunt Cait."

"I thought you would."

"Should I wrap it up again for you," Maggie asked, "or will you carry it?"

Fast as he could, Bill reached over the counter for his cat carving. *It?* Didn't she know a he-cat when she saw one?

"I'll carry him," he said. "He's not heavy."

The second his fingers closed around the silky-cool wood, he felt good inside.

Not that he could pay too much attention to the cat-god right now, Bill thought. Later, in his room with the door closed, he could look at him all he wanted.

"Hold on, Bill," Maggie said. "You'll want to read the legend behind this piece. I have the paper somewhere here. . . ." She went back to opening drawers and jangling her shells.

Aunt Cait had wandered off. Bill saw her over in a corner, fighting to unroll a big poster. It was giving her a hard time about being unrolled.

"Oh, Bill," she called out, "come over here, take a look. You'll appreciate this, I think."

When he walked over and saw the poster, he knew what she meant. There, drawn bigger than life-size, was the cat-god. Also on the poster were two other wood carvings, a deer's head and a pelican's head.

Written at the top of the poster was "Art Is Timeless," exactly what Aunt Cait had said about the sunrise this morning on the sandbar. Bill wanted the poster. Now, if he could only get her to buy it for him.

Not that he thought she wouldn't. Whenever he asked Mom nicely, she always would. Dad too. In fact, Mom and Dad would usually buy anything for him no matter how he asked. He guessed he had nagged for stuff a few times.

Maybe if he pretended to expect Aunt Cait to buy it for him, she would. Bill figured it was worth a try.

"I'd like that to hang in my room," he said.

"It *would* look wonderful," she admitted. "Did you bring any money with you, Bill?"

He stared at her. "Money?"

"That's what I said. The poster was donated to the art league by the artist to help with fund raising. Unframed like this, it costs twenty-five dollars. Do you have it?"

He studied the floor tiles. "No. I mean, not on me. At home I do. I mean, at your house I do. Dad gave me lots of spending money."

His aunt's face looked calm as could be, but her voice sounded funny.

"I see. But you *do* want to buy the poster?"

"Definitely."

"Tell you what, then, Bill. When I pay for your gift, I'll lay out the money for the poster. When we get home, you'll reimburse me. How does that sound?"

It sounded tough, but what could he do? Bill guessed he shouldn't have expected her to buy him the poster and the cat-god too. It could be *he* was the one who'd been tough.

"Sure," he said in what he hoped was a decent, good-kid voice. "No problem. Thanks again, Aunt Cait."

Back at the counter Maggie handed him a sheet of paper. "This goes with the cat-god. I'd read it right away if I were you, Bill. Especially read the part about the cat-god being dangerous in the wrong hands."

He stared up at her. *Dangerous?*

"I also wanted to tell you," she said, "about the Calusa craft class I'm teaching. It's a six-week course, and the first class is this Friday night, seven to nine. I think you'll like it. I couldn't help noticing how interested you are in my shell jewelry. You could make some for yourself."

Bill backed away. "I don't think—"

"*Or* you could copy King Calos's jewelry," she said. "And you might try to copy his turban too. I have a hatbox full of feathers crying to be used." Maggie winked. "How about it? I'd *love* to have you in my class."

"Okay," he said, amazed at himself. Still, in case that television set never turned up, it would give him something interesting to do one night a week. "I'll have to check with Aunt Cait, though."

He saw her thumbing through the pages of a book and decided against asking her right away. Instead, he headed for the main gallery and sat down on a stone bench with his back to the king's portrait. He didn't need those powerful spirit eyes staring at him.

Unfolding the paper titled "Legend of the Key Marco Cat-god," Bill began to read: "The cat-god statue was carved minus fangs and claws in order to limit its powers of retaliation. While the Calusas believed they had a strong spiritual connection with the proud panther, they also believed that their panther-god statue could become dangerous in the wrong hands."

Reading the words, Bill loosened his grip on his cat-god so fast he nearly dropped it. One thing he did know about cats was that they hated being held too tight.

He went on. "The Calusas also believed the carved cat deity could come to life whenever and wherever it chose to do so."

Also, according to the paper, the cat-god was "a

manlike being in the guise of a panther." That was *really* strange.

Anyway, he thought, what was he worrying about? This little carving was only a copycat, not the real one from almost fourteen hundred years ago.

Only a copy? Hey, wait, where'd he hear that before?

After a few seconds of thinking, Bill remembered where, and a shiver rippled up along his spine. Aunt Cait had told him how much her masks hated being called copies. Which meant his cat-god statue probably wouldn't like it too much either.

"So, listen," he whispered in what he thought was a best-pal voice, "don't feel bad about having . . . well, no fangs. You ask me, you look great enough without them."

With one finger he gently traced the outline of the fangless mouth carved into the cypress wood.

"Actually," he said, "unless you're a vampire, there's not much use for fangs. They'd probably only get in your way."

Behind him King Calos laughed.

Bill jerked his head around, eyeing the king's portrait suspiciously. Or had it only been Aunt Cait laughing as she headed toward him across the gallery, his rolled-up poster in her hand?

7.

The Swamp Tracker

"Evenin'."

Startled out of his doze, Bill jerked upright in his chair. The last he remembered he'd been sitting on the lanai after supper, watching the sun sink into the Gulf.

He leaned forward to see better. It couldn't be. He knew it couldn't be. But with the light streaming from the house outlining the dark head and wide shoulders, whoever it was standing in the doorway looked like King Calos!

The candlelight on the table was bright enough for him to make out a strong jutting nose and chin, high cheekbones, and glittering dark eyes.

"I'm late, sorry, couldn't be helped."

The deep, mellow voice *sounded* all right. Bill sat up straighter, his fingers fiercely gripping the wooden arms of the deck chair.

"That's okay," he whispered.

The mysterious dark figure moved toward him across the lanai.

"Glad to meet you, Bill. I'm Grant Oscee."

"Ohh," he said, jolting to his feet when the man reached out to shake his hand. "I thought—I mean, in the dark you look like someone else I know."

"Who's that?"

"I don't exactly *know* him," Bill explained. "Can't. He's been dead too long."

Grant laughed. "That's a new one."

"I mean, you look like this Calusa king I saw in a painting at the art league."

"Calos? That *is* a compliment. Funny you should say that, Bill. For the past few days, while I was in the mangrove swamps, I've been feeling close to my ancestors. In fact, whenever I spend time in the Glades, I feel that way."

Grant pulled out a chair and sat down at the table. Bill did the same.

"Ancestors? You mean you really *are* related to King Calos?"

"My last name—Oscee? The greatest Seminole chief of all time in Florida was Osceola. He was a mixed-blood: Creek and Scots. I'm a mixed-blood too. Father's an Irishman. I follow tradition, taking my mother's name. She's Miccosukee."

"Wow," he said.

"And far back? Yes, Bill, I do have some Calusa blood still singing in my veins."

Bill stared across the table at the silver streaks in

Grant Oscee's thick black hair. His hair was long, but not long enough to hide the tiny white shell stuck in his earlobe. In a white open-necked shirt with the sleeves rolled up, he looked lean, brown . . . hammer-strong.

When Grant didn't show up on time for dinner, Aunt Cait had insisted they hold off eating, saying she was sure he'd be along at any moment. But after nearly an hour had passed, she'd given up, and they'd eaten supper without him.

"I only hope he's not in trouble," she'd said. "Even for an experienced swamp tracker like Grant, the Everglades can be treacherous."

"What could happen?" he'd wanted to know.

"If you don't mind, Bill, I'd rather not think about the many possibilities. I'm going inside to straighten up the kitchen, get my mind off my worries. You sit, relax, enjoy the sunset."

That had been okay with him. Now, looking across the table at Grant, Bill wondered why Aunt Cait had even worried a second.

She came onto the lanai carrying a pitcher of iced tea and a plate loaded with cheese and crackers. He saw her teeth flash as she smiled. "Did you tell Bill why you were delayed?"

"Definitely my fault," Grant said. "Should've known better than to sing romantic ballads in that particular waterway. Next thing I knew, a love-sick gator was trying to climb into my dugout canoe. Worst of it was, I lost my paddle. Ever been up a creek without a paddle, Bill?"

"Is that *really* true?"

"Swampies don't lie, they just tell tales."

For the next half hour Bill listened to swamp tales that made the hairs on his legs go on red alert.

Grant's tales were all about Glades creatures: spiders the size of dinner plates, with webs so huge they stretched from tree to tree; strange birds and bugs and apple snails. Grant told him tales about snakes too: indigos, cottonmouths, rattlers, corals.

"Ever see a bobcat?" Bill asked.

"Sure, many times. Saw one on this porch when I was building the house. Bobcat looked right through the kitchen window at me. It screamed a couple of times, then left."

Bill sat up straighter. On this porch? Did that mean his panther might only be a bobcat?

"How about panthers, Grant? Ever see any?"

The swamp tracker leaned back in his chair, folded his arms, and took a deep breath. "Panthers? Now you're talking! Would you like to hear some panther tales, Bill?"

"Guess I would," he admitted.

"I grew up in the Glades, and even now I'm there at least one weekend a month. Yet I can count on the fingers of one hand the times I've seen a panther up close. Loners, they are, elusive, smart. I've heard things, though, over the years."

"Like what?"

"For one thing, how they feel for kids, especially lost kids. Panthers seem to have a kind of bond, or call it a feeling of kinship, with small, helpless humans. Quite a few cases where a family is camping out in the Glades, and a kid wanders off and gets lost. Story always goes, the lost kid is scared, crying, hiding under a tree, the perfect prey. Well, night falls, and a panther shows up. The big cat keeps watch all night, keeps the bears, wild boar, and the reptiles away until morning . . . until rescue comes."

"That's only a tale, right," Bill asked, "not really true?"

"Might think so," Grant said. "Might think the kids were making up stories. But the proof always comes from the panther itself—tracks, scat, claw marks on the mangrove tree roots."

"Got any more tales about panthers?"

"Matter of fact, I do. One I think you'll like goes—"

"Hold that story." Aunt Cait set a plate loaded with food on the table in front of Grant. "Eat first."

Bill sighed. If only she could've waited awhile longer.

"What a pal," Grant said. "Thanks, Cait."

She grinned. "I'm just glad you made it back in one piece."

"Wait until I'm finished eating, Bill," he said, "and I'll tell you about the white panther."

"The white panther? Okay!"

"Glades folks call it Manther," Grant added.

The telephone rang. Aunt Cait got up to answer it, and Bill sat back to watch every bite Grant put in his mouth.

"You want to come in here, Bill?" Aunt Cait yelled. "It's your mother on the phone, calling from Helsinki."

As Bill shoved back his chair, his heart began to thud. Mom . . . Dad . . . they hadn't forgotten him after all.

His mother's voice sounded hollow, as if she were talking to him over an intercom.

"Mom, guess what," he said. "At Aunt Cait's house? A panther, Mom, I saw a panther!"

There! It felt great saying his secret out loud to someone.

"Sweetheart, a panther?" She laughed. "But why should I be surprised? I remember Cait telling me she had a sphinx in her living room. Listen, honey, where we are is so—"

But the second Bill heard her say "panther," then "sphinx" in that teasy, airy voice of hers, the doors in his ears slammed shut. Mom didn't believe him, that's all he knew. She didn't even care.

The faint words he could hear were all *her* stuff, hers and Dad's, boring little word-balls he didn't want to catch. Who cares, Bill thought, about "Finland . . . hotel . . . business . . . delightful people"?

"Did you hear me, luv? How are *you*?"

Like she really wants to know, he thought.

"Billy? Honey? Are you still there?"

"Yes," he muttered, blinking back tears. *Where does she think I am, New Jersey?* "Mom, don't call me Billy, call me Bill," he said. "That's what everyone here calls me."

"All right, *Bill,*" she said, "I'll put your father on now. He's so anxious to talk to you. We'll call you again from Stockholm, how's that?"

"Okay," he whispered. "Bye, Mom."

"I'm glad you're having a nice time," she said.

Where'd she get that idea?

"Son, it's Dad. What's up?"

Blinking his eyes open and closed to dry off the lashes, Bill kept count of his blinks so he wouldn't have to catch any of his father's word-balls. Who cared about either of them? They could phone again from Sweden or from one of Saturn's rings and he wouldn't care.

"Can't . . . really . . . hear . . . you, Dad," he droned softly in his best humanoid voice. "You . . . are . . . fading . . . out."

It worked. Dad gave up. Bill stopped blinking his eyes at a count of sixty-three. By the time he'd put the receiver back in its cradle, his lashes were stone dry. Good, he could go back to the lanai without looking like a bleary-eyed baby.

He'd forgotten about the masks. Lined up on the wall, twenty-four faces were looking right at him.

"Who cares what you think?" he told them. "You're all nothing."

But walking along the hall to the lanai, he was sorry about what he'd said. He knew how it felt hanging around a house, day after day, feeling like nothing.

Since he'd been gone, Aunt Cait and Grant had made themselves comfortable in loungers. The loungers were pulled close together, and the middle one was empty, waiting for him.

They weren't talking. Instead they were peacefully watching the Marco moonlight clear a straight silver path along the canal.

Bill settled himself on the middle lounger as quietly as he could.

8.

Manther

Aunt Cait's potted plants were huddled together near the mesh screen, their big elephant-ear leaves flopping every which way. Nighttime on the lanai was great, Bill thought. It was like being outdoors without the bugs.

He sat quietly on the middle lounger until Grant broke the silence.

"Bill, ever hear a baby cry?"

The unexpected question made him laugh. "Guess so, sure."

"Ever hear a woman scream?"

"Mom on a bad day, or Mrs. Fledsoe, our housekeeper, when she sings along with the vacuum cleaner."

"An opera singer?" Grant asked.

"Not exactly," Bill said. "Mrs. Fledsoe's voice would wreck an opera."

"Or the sound cold water makes hitting red-hot coals? The shrill whine of a wood sander? The smooth purr of a new car motor?"

Bill wrinkled his forehead. "What do car motors and wood sanders have to do with anything?"

"What I'm talking about are the many sounds panthers make," Grant explained, "the panther sounds I personally know about."

"You know a panther personally, Grant?"

"No. Heard them, though, many times. I've heard panthers mew like newborn kittens, squeak like mice, roar, whistle, hiss, wail like banshees, cough, and sing soprano."

Okay! Grant said panthers coughed. That meant it *had* been a panther on the porch. He felt better. Not a bobcat, a panther!

"But I'll tell you"—Grant's head rested against the cushioned back of the lounger; with his arms crossed over his chest and the moon painting silver designs all over his face, he looked so much like the Calusa king, Bill couldn't stop staring at him—"there's no other sound in the Glades to equal the wild, keening sadness of a panther's scream at night." Grant sighed. "The sound of that eerie night scream pierces right through me, makes my hair rise, brings tears to my eyes. That scream is lodged in my soul forever. I'll never forget it."

Seconds passed, piling up to a minute. Bill was glad for the pause. He needed time to imagine the skin-piercing scream for himself. Harder to imagine, though, was Grant with tears in his eyes.

"I'm going to leave you two," Aunt Cait said. "Grant, you'll excuse me, but I *have* heard the Manther tale before, and I'm so sleepy, my eyes won't stay open. I'll just toddle off to bed."

"Toddle, Cait?" Grant laughed. "Like to see that."

"Watch, then," she said.

By the time Aunt Cait got herself up and off the lounger, Bill couldn't help laughing too. She did a great imitation of someone sleepier, older, and weirder than she already was.

"Nighty-night," she croaked in an ancient, crusty voice. "Don't stay up too late. Remember, we all have a dig date in the morning."

"Okay," he said, "good night, Aunt Cait." He looked back at Grant. "*You're* coming to the dig tomorrow?"

"I work with the team whenever I can," he said, "and I'm hoping to put in lots of time at the dig this summer. Besides, as a favor to my good friend Ryan—Annie's dad—I'll be picking her up mornings and bringing her home afternoons."

Lucky Annie.

"So, Bill," Grant began, "when you get to swapping tales with Glades folk, you hear the same tale told in many different ways. This particular tale happened a hundred years ago, or—depending on who's telling the tale—much earlier. Then, again, I've heard it happened only twenty years ago. Anyway, Bill, here's what happened, whenever."

His voice dropped to a deeper tone. "Most tellers do agree where it happened: way, way back, in the deepest, most secret heart of the Glades. If you knew the Glades as I do, Bill, that could be anywhere you happen to find yourself.

"So, there was this young woman, a girl actually, though she was already a wife and the new mother of a baby son.

"She wasn't happy this day I'm talking about. No, grief stricken is what she was, and for good reason. Seems her husband was gone, never to return from his hunt in the Glades. It had been two, three days since he'd left, and his wife knew what she feared most was true, her husband was dead.

"Some said later he was set upon by a pack of wild boar. Some said he was dragged down a gator hole. One swampie said, for a fact, it was quicksand that got him."

Quicksand in the Glades? Bill shivered.

"She was scared half to death," Grant said, "this poor young mother left alone and defenseless with her brand-new infant in a dinky little cabin deep in the swamps.

"Stark terrified, she was, crying her heart out, wondering what she'd ever do now with no one to fend for her.

"See, Bill, she wasn't born to the Glades, she'd come there only for the love of her man, and now what? She hadn't a clue how to survive, or how to get back to civilization. There wasn't any food in the cabin, nor a weapon to protect her babe from all the wild, growling terrors lurking outside.

"She cried until night fell, and the rains came, lightning and thunder, and, they say, she kept on crying in fear and desperation. The baby? Good little thing apparently, sleeping peacefully in his cradle while his mother wept."

Man, Bill thought, *I'd cry too. I'd keep crying even after all my tears got used up. I bet even Cory Barrister would be crying if he was in her shoes.*

"Can't you just see it, Bill? Hear it too. Pitch-dark, rain thrumming hard outside on the rickety pineboard porch, thunder booming and cracking, daggers of lightning stabbing at that flimsy cabin roof.

"The girl wasn't looking out at the storm. Even if she had been, by this time she would've been nearly blind from so much crying, wouldn't you say, Bill?"

"Definitely," he agreed hastily.

"Which is exactly why she wouldn't have noticed eyes peering at her through the window. And since she was sobbing so loudly, she wouldn't have heard the scratchings or the powerful thrusts and pushings at the cabin door.

"No," Grant said, "that poor weeping young woman didn't hear a blessed thing until—*until the door splintered and burst wide open!*"

Bill did the best sit-up of his life.

"Imagine what she must've felt, looking up to see a full-grown she-panther in the doorway. Flashes of lightning outlining her clearly, thunder crashing like cymbals to announce her presence, the great golden cat sprang forward into the dim cabin, white fangs and wet fur and fierce yellow eyes gleaming."

"What'd the girl do?"

"Ever been frozen with fear, Bill? That's what she was, frozen stiff, lock-jawed, lock-limbed with shock and fear. She couldn't move a muscle even when the she-panther streaked across the tiny room, snatched her precious baby from his cradle, and carried him, bed-clothes and all, back out through the open doorway."

"Oh, no," he whispered, "not the baby."

"And I'm sure that's exactly what she said, 'Oh, no, God, no please, not my baby.'

"Only then did the mother jump up from her chair and race out onto the rain-flooded porch. She must've stood there, gripping the porch rail, screaming after the she-cat. She must've screamed 'til she was hoarse.

"But way out there, if any human did have an ear tuned to her scream, he'd have thought it the cry of the panther, so sorrowful, lonely, and full of despair did it sound over the raging storm."

"What happened to the baby?"

"The baby boy was lost, forever, never to be seen again. At least, some say that." His voice sank to a husky whisper. "Some tell it different, though. Some say the boy *was* seen again, many times."

Bill leaned forward, watching wide-eyed as Grant calmly picked up his glass of iced tea and drank.

"Some years later, so the story goes, a white panther was spotted walking the Glades. Those who claimed to see the creature close up said the white panther didn't have a tail or fur, just a tangled yellow mane. Said he was naked, walking the swamps on his hind legs like a man.

"Swampies called him ghost cat or the man-panther. After a while the name got to be Manther."

"Manther," Bill repeated softly.

"Yes, and even today you'll hear someone swear they've seen Manther."

"Today?" he gasped. "You mean Manther could be walking around naked right now?"

"Who really knows? The tale was told to me when I was a boy, younger than you. I remember being out in the Glades thinking about that baby boy, wondering about him, wishing I could *be* him. Thought he was lucky." Grant laughed. "Call me a hopeless case, but I suppose I still think that."

"Lucky?" Bill stared at the swamp tracker with disbelief. "How come?"

"Oh, just for the privilege of knowing a panther as none of us humans ever will. Think how it'd be, raised to adulthood, or mantherhood, in all the wild, secret ways of the panther."

Whew! Bill slumped back against the lounger cushions. Maybe Grant liked the idea of getting kidnapped and ending up half-panther, half-man, but he—

The words printed on the paper that had come with his cat-god statue flashed clearly into his mind: "man-like being in the guise of a panther."

"The Key Marco Cat-god," he blurted excitedly, "he's a Manther, right, Grant? The cat-god's from the year 600, so that means panthers probably stole Calusa kids too!"

"Calusa kids? Fact is, Bill, Calusa kids—just about

your age—went far out of their way to get adopted by panthers, eagles, wolves, deer, alligators, you name it."

"They *wanted* to get adopted by alligators?"

"It was part of growing up. Young Calusas had to spend time in the Glades by themselves, fasting, praying, waiting to be—I'll use the word again—adopted. It's called a vision quest, or, as some tribes call it, crying for a vision."

"Vision?" Bill asked. "You mean—"

But Grant was already halfway off his lounger.

"Looks like we'll have to continue our conversation another time, Bill. It's late and we both have to be up early. Tell you what, how about making plans for a day in the Glades?"

The Glades?

"No fangs! I mean, no thanks. Aunt Cait needs me at the dig and—"

"Don't worry, I'll talk to her," he said. "And when we get to the Glades, I'll tell you more about crying for a vision. You'll get to see exactly *where* Calusa kids did it. You really shouldn't let the summer go by without seeing the Glades. There's no other place like it."

"Okay," he whispered.

"Great," Grant said, reaching out to shake his hand, man to man. "We'll go in a couple of weeks. How's that?"

"Fine," Bill said, "sounds good to me."

But when the front door closed, Bill didn't feel fine. It didn't help that Aunt Cait was upstairs asleep and he was downstairs all alone. In bed he arranged the sheet so every bit of his hair spikes was covered. In that dark, secret undercover space, he whispered into a tiny, pointed cypress ear.

"I'm scared, Manther. I'm scared to death of those Glades."

Ashamed, Bill clutched his only pal, wishing with all his heart he was a different, braver kid or, even better, a panther-cub kid who walked around wild and naked and free.

In the last second before he fell asleep, away from the scary world, he was sure he heard the cat-god statue whispering back to him: "It's all right, Bill. I'm here. We'll think of something."

9.

A Charred Discovery

Bill watched as Grant rowed his dinghy toward the Horr's Island shore. "Where's Annie?" he yelled. "I thought you were picking her up this morning."

With a final heave of the oars, Grant skimmed the small boat through the shallows onto the wet sand. "I thought so too," he said, "but her grandmother's taking her to Fort Myers for a couple of days. I tell you, Bill, Annie didn't look happy. You'll miss her, huh?"

"Miss *Annie*? *Me*? I hardly even know Annie."

"That's right, I forgot. You've only been here a few days."

"Four," Bill said. "Actually, three and a half."

Grant stood gazing across the sunlit water to where his sailboat, the *Marco Polo*, was anchored. "Annie's a good kid," he said. "I've known her since the day she was born."

"Aunt Cait knew *me* when I was a baby," he said, "but I only met her last week when she came to pick me up. All I knew about her was what my parents told me and what I could tell from her postcards. She's been everywhere, all over the world, I guess."

"Cait and I go back a long way too. Lots of adventures, digs, and fun in faraway places." Grant laughed. "First time I met her, in the Himalayas, she was dangling from a rope off the side of a cliff. It was her first time mountain climbing, and she was a nervous wreck. I was the guide on that trek. When I finished talking her up that peak, she wasn't afraid anymore.

"Fact is, she couldn't be afraid and determined to survive at the same time. Remember that, if you ever find yourself in a similar situation. Concentrate on another idea or emotion. Focus your mind and, presto, your fear will go. It works."

"Okay," he said, trailing Grant across the sand toward the shell mound, "if you say so."

During the long drive to Florida, Aunt Cait had told him the Himalayan story. She'd said when a person saves another person's life, they're connected forever. *And that's the way it is with everyone here,* Bill thought. *They're all connected and I'm not.*

His mother always said, if he wanted friends at school, he had to reach out and make an effort once in a while. He remembered getting so mad after one of her pep talks, he'd told her she sounded like a telephone company commercial. Maybe his mother was right, though.

"Grant," he said, running to catch up, "only reason I sort of miss Annie is because I had something great to show her. Want to see it?"

"Absolutely."

He couldn't wait to show Grant his shell and find out for sure whether it was a genuine dwarf queen conch. Bill reached around to slap his own backpack. "It's right here. Soon as we get to the site, okay?"

Later, climbing up the mound, he congratulated himself. Not a bad start, telling Grant that he missed Annie. That took guts.

But when they reached the site and he was unsnapping his backpack, Aunt Cait started shouting. Bill dropped his pack on the ground beneath a tree and hurried over to her.

She was so excited, her blue eyes were shooting out sparks. "Look down there, you two," she said. "Tell me what you see."

Bill peered into the pit. "A box? What's a big box like that doing down there?"

The pit was about six feet deep. The back of his neck prickled. Dead people were buried six feet under, weren't they?

"That's not a giant-sized coffin down there, is it, Aunt Cait?"

"No," Grant answered for her, "but you may be close."

"Let's just hope that slab of cypress down there is as solid as it looks," Aunt Cait said. "I was afraid to stay down there, afraid the wood might crumble under my weight. We'll have to get help bringing it up.

"Here, Bill, join me in a stick of gum."

Startled, he held out his hand.

She smiled. "And don't give me that 'You're crazy' look. You should know by now that in moments of high stress or joy, I chew."

"Um, thanks," he mumbled, wishing she'd quit reading his mind. She chewed, he counted.

"Cait," Grant said, "I've got an idea. How about we let Bill climb down there with a brush. He's light enough, and he could take a look, see if there's some kind of latching mechanism."

"Me?" Bill gulped. "What if the wood is rotten? What if it caves in while I'm down there?"

"It won't," Grant said, "because you won't stand on it. All I want you to do is climb down, hang on to the scaffolding with one hand, and do some very cautious sweeping with the other. I'm too heavy, and Cait may be too."

"Okay, okay, I'll do it." For a change being a lightweight was coming in handy.

"Only thing is, Grant . . . Aunt Cait, if I do get buried alive or something, don't wait four hundred years to dig me out."

They were both smiling when he grabbed hold of the top rung of the scaffold, swung himself around, and began to descend.

With each step down Bill felt calmer. When his feet were planted firmly on the bottom rung, he grabbed the handle of the stiff-bristled brush Grant lowered to him.

For the next few minutes Bill concentrated on cleaning the crumbly black sand away from the wood. In many places the damp sand was clumped together and he had to loosen it gradually with strokes of the brush. While he was doing this, Grant called down that he was switching on the spotlight.

Bill was glad to hear it. The pit was cool and dark and sort of spooky. His right hand was tired, so he switched the brush to his left and continued stroking at a large sand lump. A few more strokes and the lump fell apart.

"Hey," he yelled, "I found pieces of something."

"What kind of pieces, Bill?" Aunt Cait's voice was excited.

"Well . . . three cracked-apart wooden pieces and one extra one. I think I know what the extra one is."

"*What?*" she asked.

"A little oar. Oh, now I see," Bill said. "Those three broken pieces? Canoes. Stick them back together with string or glue and they'll make a miniature catamaran."

Above him Bill could hear Grant and Aunt Cait whooping and yelling. He grinned. "On two of the pieces? Paint. Oh, and on the tip of the oar and all three boat parts are burn marks. And it smells smoky down here too. Like a barbecue pit."

Hanging on to the scaffold, Bill stretched out his arm to use the brush on another section of the wooden slab. He swept the black sand aside. "You're going to like *this*," he yelled.

"What is it?" they said together.

"Carvings, a bird and a curled-up snake."

After that Bill couldn't talk much. He had to follow so many instructions, he lost track of time.

First he had to replace sand over the painted wood to keep it from disintegrating in the air. He had to put the boat pieces and oar into a pail. After he covered them with sand, he had to climb halfway up the scaffolding with one hand to pass the pail to Grant. His arms ached, but when he finished and climbed out of the pit and saw their happy faces, his aches disappeared.

"What a discovery," Aunt Cait told him. "The charred toy catamaran is wonderful! All the encouragement we need. Thanks, Bill."

Toy catamaran? he wondered.

10.

The Naturalist

"Clear the way," Annie shouted two mornings after his discovery. Her voice flew across the water to where Bill stood with Aunt Cait on the Horr's Island beach.

Annie was rowing so fast, the little boat seemed to shoot through the shallows like a fat brown arrow.

"Look at Grant." Aunt Cait laughed. "He's holding on for dear life."

Well . . . no, he wasn't, Bill decided. He couldn't imagine Grant ever worrying about a little thing like getting capsized.

When they came ashore, Aunt Cait and Grant immediately headed for the mound. Annie stayed on the beach with him. She looked different. After he stared at her awhile, he knew why.

"Hey, Annie, what happened to your emergency mosquito net?"

Scrubbing her hair with her fingers, she looked

ready to scream. "I know, I look dis-gusting, but Grandma insisted."

Bill smiled. No matter how she messed with her hair, she couldn't change the neat look of the short, springy curls. For a second he felt sorry for her. "Don't worry about it," he said. "At least you'll be cool like me."

"You sound just like Syl-via," Annie hissed. "All she kept telling me was how marvelous I'd look with all my wild-woman hair off my neck, how marvelously cool I'd feel. What I hated was hearing that word *marvelous* a million times. What I *really* hated was not having a choice about it. Know what I mean, Bill?"

"Sure," he told her, "because we're still kids, and kids don't get to choose stuff much."

Annie's face brightened. "Here, take it as a souvenir." She handed him a bug-oil bottle. "Grandma made me throw my supply in the dumpster. I saved this. See, I even sealed it up with masking tape for you."

"Thanks. Maybe it will come in handy someday." When he got back to New Jersey, he could carry the bottle in his pocket in case Cory and his gang gave him any trouble. Man, he could see Cory falling down unconscious from a single whiff.

The chugging whine of an outboard motor made them turn to look.

"Oh-oh," Annie said, "see what you started, Bill?"

"What *I* started? Who are all those people?"

"Members of the regular dig team," Annie told him. "Usually during summer they travel, lecture, or work like dogs in the lab. It takes lots longer to analyze and interpret artifacts than it does to discover them, Bill. Discovery, that's the *easy* part."

Bill laughed. "Hey, Annie, you're not jealous, are you?"

"*Moi?* Jealous? Where'd you get *that* idea, Bill? What makes you think I even care? Think I care that I've been slaving at digs since I was seven years old, then you come and in not even a week find important clues as to why some Calusas disappeared?"

"You *are* jealous, Annie. What can I tell you? I'm lucky, that's all. Hey, what important clues? The toy catamaran?"

"It was half-burned, wasn't it?" she asked. "Didn't I tell you about the Calusas that vanished overnight? It could've been because of a horrible fire. No one knows what caused the fire. It could've been lightning or enemy invaders, or the Calusas could've set the fire themselves as they escaped. . . . Thanks to you we might find more answers to why they fled and left behind all their good stuff."

She made a face. "And thanks to you it's going to be crowded here today. Let's ask if we can stay on the beach for a while. We could scout for shells or maybe call dolphins."

"Call dolphins? On the phone? They answer much?"

"Not on the phone, silly. What you do is call to dolphins with your mind. They hear, I *know* they do, but they come only if they feel like it. If they're not doing something better."

"Sure, Annie," he said, "if you really want to."

"Oh, I *do*," Annie wailed, "I need to feel free. It was awful having to hang out at hair salons and boutiques. At night I had to dress up and eat at weird restaurants. One looked like the Addams family house."

She sat down hard on the sand. "I'm a born naturalist, and naturalists belong outdoors. I wish Sylvia would understand that and stop trying to change me all around."

"I'm just the opposite," he said. "I like being indoors best, but Aunt Cait keeps me outdoors too much."

After introductions to the visitors were over, and they'd gotten permission to stay on the beach, Bill remembered his queen conch. With all the excitement two days ago, he hadn't had a chance to show it to Grant.

"Sit right here, Annie," he said, "don't move. I want to show you something cool."

He ran across the sand to where he'd left his backpack. Unsnapping the front pocket as he ran back toward Annie, he spotted sea-grape leaves scattered near the bushes. One of those big saucer-shaped leaves would make a great display pad for his shell.

Bill dropped his pack on the sand near Annie and headed for the bushes. "I'll be right back," he shouted. "Remember, don't move."

"Don't worry, Bill," she said in a strange voice, "I'm definitely not moving now."

"What do you mean *now*?"

She pointed at the sand, her green eyes bigger than

sea-grape leaves. *"That's* what you wanted to show me?"

Bill looked. He saw Manther's small face peeking out from a corner of his backpack. And he saw—

"Oh, no," he whispered, "not another one."

Slithering slowly from the pocket of his pack was a small black- yellow- and red-striped snake.

"How'd that get in there?" he croaked.

He knew how. "Two days ago," he said, "I was going to show Grant my shell, then Aunt Cait started yelling and— Hey, Annie, what kind of snake is it?"

It was pretty small, so probably it was harmless, Bill thought. Glancing at Annie's face, though, he changed his mind.

"It's d-deadly?" he asked.

"It's a coral . . . member of the cobra family. A burrower, so it probably loved your backpack. A chewer too."

"A chewer?" He wrapped his arms around his middle and held himself tightly.

"Corals don't have fangs," she said. "They latch on to the skin between your fingers and start chewing. They never let go either, they chew and chew and—"

"Stop!"

The snake picked up speed, racing toward the path that led up to the mound.

"We'd better warn them when we go up later, Bill."

"Don't say it came from my pack. Aunt Cait will have a fit. She warned me never, ever to leave it unsnapped outdoors."

"Good thing you didn't unsnap your pack *indoors,"*

she said. "Think about it, Bill. While you were asleep, it could've—"

"*Knock it off!*"

Bill shut his eyes. Two snakes and a scorpion in a week!

When he opened his eyes, Annie was standing in front of him.

"I'm sorry," she said. "I shouldn't have done that to you. See, I'm still mad at Sylvia. Since I can't say anything to her, you got my meanness. That wasn't a deadly coral, it was a king snake. It's harmless. But if you see one—"

"I know," Bill said, "don't put my fingers in small spaces and don't step up, onto, or down off of a ledge or a log without checking first." He sighed. "Aunt Cait told me. There's tons of bad stuff to remember around here. Snakes—how come they like me so much? I hate them!"

"Don't say that," she said. "If you think about it, snakes have it tough. Most people do hate them, so snakes are always getting rotten vibrations buzzing through the air at them. It makes them, you know, sort of defensive and testy."

"Worse than testy," he muttered. "They bite or chew you to death."

"Not if you treat them nice," Annie said. "When I'm around places snakes live and I see one, I usually keep my distance. I explain what I'm doing, ask it if it minds me being there. I say nice things to make up for all the awful things they hear.

"Once I even told a five-foot indigo he was gorgeous." She laughed. "He *was* gorgeous, but he got all embarrassed and took off into the bushes."

Bill shook his head. "You and Aunt Cait, you're both nutso. You talk to snakes, she talks to her plants. She even talks to her salad greens!"

"What's nutso about that? Trees and plants and flowers *love* attention. All living things love music, did you know that? Play good music for dolphins and they'll do a water ballet."

"Annie, ever think about trying out for *Jeopardy!*?"

"Sure, but I'm too young yet. Listen, I have a big favor to ask you. A really huge favor, I guess, but you could end up liking it."

Bill didn't like the sound of her voice.

"Sylvia signed me up for a six-week evening class at the art league. It starts Friday. It's a Calusa crafts class and it sounds kind of fun, but I'll probably be the only kid there. Come with me, *please?*"

He looked away. "If I do you that big favor, you have to do one for me."

"Anything," she said, "*anything.*"

"If I go to the classes with you, you have to go to the Glades with me. Grant invited me to go in a couple of weeks."

"Deal." Annie stuck out her hand and they shook on it.

Bill burst out laughing. "I hate to tell you this, Annie, but I already *am* signed up for that crafts class."

She only shrugged. "A deal's a deal."

A moment later he heard their names being shouted. Whoever was calling to them from the edge of the path

leading up to the mound sounded excited. "Annie—
Bill—come up now. Another discovery—*incredible!*"

They ran.

But at the site no one was talking. As Grant and three
members of the team slowly pulled the heavy cypress
slab from the pit, the other people appeared to be holding their breath.

Bill glanced at Aunt Cait's face. How could she look
so calm and serious? Wasn't this the important
moment she'd been waiting for? Shouldn't she, and
Grant too, be smiling?

He nudged Annie. "Why is everyone so gloomy? Like
it's a funeral or something?"

She was on her hands and knees, as close as she
could get to the edge of the excavation. "They're not
gloomy, they're excited, but it sort of *is* a funeral, Bill,"
she whispered. "Look down there."

He looked. What he thought he saw was a small red
human-faced mask topped with shiny-black braids.
Dozens of those skinny braids. Below the mask he saw
a beautiful triple-strand necklace of painted shells and
white feathers.

He gasped. It wasn't a mask, it was a *face.* Wrapped
in animal skins, curled up in a nest of shells and Spanish moss was a—kid! *A mummy kid!*

He stepped back and sat down hard on the ground.
What was a kid his size doing buried there in the
dirt?

An image of the charred, broken toy catamaran
flashed in his mind. *It's the mummy kid's toy,* he
thought.

Annie was a few feet away, still kneeling near the edge of the pit.

"That's rotten, Annie," Bill said, "rotten!"

"Not rotten," she said over her shoulder, "well preserved. Tannin from the mangrove roots makes a great preservative. So does sand. That's why the paint and wood and his skin stayed so good. At least his face did. See it? Like soft red leather and—"

"*Stop*," he said. "I don't want to hear your scientific talk. He's just a kid like us. Doesn't anyone care about that?"

The team members bustled around above and below in the pit, doing their chores. Bill couldn't stand being around people who could laugh and say stuff like "Fantastic find!" and "Good work!"

Because look at that poor red-faced kid down there, all cramped up in a hole, alone and forgotten for who knew how many years.

"Why *is* his face painted red?" Bill asked Annie.

Annie didn't answer, but Aunt Cait did as she sat down beside him. "For many cultures even now," she said quietly, "red is the color of life."

"*Life?*" Bill snorted. "That's dumb. He's dead, isn't he? Who put him there, anyway? What'd he die from?"

"The ancients believed in the survival of the soul after physical death," Aunt Cait explained, "so they painted his face to express their belief that his life would go on in another form.

"Sealed in the tomb, the boy became an important link to the Afterworld and the Great Spirit. Until all the lab tests are done, we won't know for sure, but from what I see so far, I'd say the boy is of royal blood. Could be the son of a cacique."

"King Calos? That kid could be his son?"

"Oh, I doubt that," Aunt Cait answered. "From the looks of things I'd say this mummy dates back long before Calos's time. I've seen Incan sacrifices to the sun-god in the high Andes that look like this. Which, of course, might prove—"

"Sacrifices to the sun-god? You mean they killed this kid on purpose to give to the *sun?*"

Aunt Cait sighed. "The sacrifice of a cacique's child was thought to bring high honor to the royal family and their descendants. They depended on the sun for everything. It was sacred, life and death to them. They wanted to please the sun, so they gave it valuable gifts. Yes, Bill, often those gifts were young people.

"This mummy could even have been sacrificed in another location and brought there to be entombed as a sacred relic. We don't know yet."

"See, Annie," Bill muttered, "didn't I tell you kids don't get to choose much? I bet this kid didn't *choose* to get sacrificed."

"Maybe he did," Annie said. "He could've felt proud and important being a link for his people."

"I doubt it."

"Bill," Aunt Cait said, "we'll make sure to talk about this later. I know you're sad and upset, but remember, when we come across beliefs and practices like this, we don't have to agree with them. We learn from the past so we won't repeat the same mistakes."

"I'm *not* upset," Bill said, "I'm *not* sad, I'm *mad!*"

After Aunt Cait left his side to do her work, Bill watched a tall bearded man taking one photograph after another of the mummy. Every time a camera flash went off, the image of the boy burned deeper in his mind.

Several minutes later the bearded man stood grinning down at him. "I'm Jon Stein from the *Eagle*," he said. "I've taken your picture, and I'll ask your aunt to sign a release. What I hope for is a comment from you. Our readers will find it interesting to hear what you have to say since you're about the same age as the mummy."

"What *I* have to say is sacrifices stink," Bill said. "No kid *ever* wants it to happen to him, no matter what *any-one* says. If a kid wants to be a link, he can do it without getting dead before he wants to be."

He put his head down on his arms. "That's all."

"Thanks, Bill. Carven's the last name? With an *n?* I wouldn't want to spell it wrong."

"Thanks," Bill said. Right now he wanted only to be left alone. Later, though, he felt something brushing against his neck. Another scorpion? Bill reached up and his fingers made contact with—

"Hey, Annie, get your mosquito net off my neck, will you?"

It was the last thing he needed, her curly head on his shoulder.

11.

Hearts & Crafts

"Only thing is," Bill said, "I can't sew."

Annie made a face. "You haven't tried yet. You're good at everything else you try in this class. Better than me."

"Wrong," he said. "Anyway, go ask Maggie if she has more fabric paints. I hope she does, we're running out."

"Ask her yourself," she whispered. "She's headed our way."

Bill heard her coming. Shells clacking, Maggie hurried toward the worktable he shared with Annie and old Mrs. Webster. Her arms were piled high with books and cardboard boxes.

"Look through these, you two," she said. "The book with the yellow cover has photos of Calusa masks and shell jewels. And here—extra tubes of paint and more feathers to share. Now—who's first?"

"First?" he asked.

"You want to start your capes tonight, don't you?"

"Bill, you'd better go first," Annie said. "It's your suede cloth. Oops—" She slapped her forehead. "I *mean*, genuine Glades deerskin."

Before class tonight he'd found a tan dress of Aunt Cait's in a box in his closet. The dress looked like deerskin and felt like it too. Bill had known instantly what he wanted to do with it.

Aunt Cait had been pleased. "That old thing? Take it. A King Calos cape is a wonderful idea. And I think you're right, the skirt is big enough for two capes, one for you, one for Annie."

Maggie was thrilled with his idea. She had sent him off to the art gallery for another study of the king's portrait. Two classes ago, when he'd decided to make a feathered turban, she'd made him do the same thing.

The turban wasn't finished yet, but thanks to Maggie's fresh supply of feathers and paints, it would be soon. Even half-done, it was the greatest thing he'd ever made, Bill thought. With the turban on he stood seven feet tall!

"Okay." He shoved back his chair. "I'll go first. What should I do?"

Dragging giant scissors from her smock pocket, Maggie held them aloft. With a wicked-witch smile she sliced and resliced the air with the blades.

"Climb on the table, Bill, drape the cloth over your shoulders, and I'll cut it down to size."

From the tabletop he had a great view of the studio.

At the long table to his right, the ex-FBI agent Joe Clemmons was gluing bits of oyster shells onto an oval mirror frame. Seated next to him, glamorous Mrs. Heggan formed pink shell pieces into a perfect rose.

At their first class three weeks ago, Mrs. Heggan had announced she planned to make two dozen shell-rose napkin rings. "Bor-ing," Annie had whispered.

Flashes from Joe's mirror hit Bill in the eye as Maggie snip-snipped the excess fabric from the bottom of his cape. "Turn, please," she instructed. "I'm almost done."

"*My* medicine-woman cape has to have lots of pockets," Annie said below him, "to hold all my healing herbs and potions. Maggie, did Calusas know about pockets in the sixteenth century?"

"Look it up," Bill said. "Maybe it's in one of those books."

"Oh, you," she said. "It doesn't have to be *so* authentic, you know. I can improvise, can't I?"

"No!" he insisted. "True Calusa or nothing, Annie."

Climbing down from the table, Bill caught ninety-two-year-old Mrs. Webster watching him. "What is it?" he whispered.

"You'll have to hem that cape and sew on the shells," Mrs. Webster told him. "If you like, I'll show you how."

"Hey, thanks!"

"On one condition," she continued. "I'll teach you to sew if you'll help me with my coquina shell earrings. The shells are so small. I've been trying to make the holes, but I can't get the hang of it. I've noticed how well you work."

"It's a deal," he said. Actually he *was* proud of learning to bore holes Calusa style with the sharpened point of a shell. Probably that was what Annie had meant when she'd said he was good at everything he tried.

While Annie was up on the table having her cape shortened, Mrs. Webster motioned him closer again. "To be truly authentic," she whispered, "you'd have to use deer sinew or palm fibers and a bone needle to sew your cape."

"Guess I'd better improvise?"

"Exactly," she said. "A good steel needle and a spool of tan cotton thread and we're in business."

Later, at Aunt Cait's house, he guessed he was in business too—finally. "You mean it?" he asked. "You actually *found* your TV set? Where was it?"

"I only remembered a few minutes ago," she said. "It's late, Bill, are you sure you want to watch television *now*?"

"Aunt Cait," he said, "does the sun rise in the east? Are shells skeletons? Yes."

"Oh, Bill, have you missed it terribly?"

"At home," he admitted, "that's practically all I ever did. Videos, video games, or I'd flip around the channels, put pieces of movies together to make a new one. Ever do that?"

She smiled. "I can't say that I have."

"So where is it?" he asked.

"On a high shelf, still in its packing crate, in the laundry room."

Bill grinned. "All right!"

A while later, halfway through the first sitcom, Aunt Cait dozed off. During the second program he almost did. Still, toddling off to bed, Bill felt great. TV! His summer was saved.

For the next few nights, right after supper, Bill watched TV. With the remote snug in his hand, he'd click around the channels the way he always had. Then—*wham*—his mind would fill up with thoughts about King Calos, an ancient Calusa symbol he wanted to paint on his cape, or the shell earring like Grant's he planned to make at his next crafts class.

After those few nights of fighting with his brain, Bill gave up TV watching temporarily. Besides, he sort of missed sitting with Aunt Cait on the lanai, watching the sun set beyond the canal.

Also, the yellow book Maggie had lent him was loaded with great information he needed to know to make Calos's costume look authentic. While Aunt Cait read or wrote up her daily dig notes, he did research and wrote in his own new field notebook, the one he'd bought with his own money at Publix two weeks ago.

The next Wednesday, though, the day the weekly edition of the *Eagle* came out, his good mood ended.

"Why'd they put *me* on the front page?" he asked Aunt Cait. "I hate it!"

The illustration filling half of the front page was two photos, side by side, one of him, one of the mummy kid. *Gross!*

The headline was gross too: *"NEW JERSEY YOUNG-*

STER MEETS ANCIENT COUNTERPART AT HORR'S ISLAND DIG."

He read the first paragraph of the news story, then handed it back to Aunt Cait. "Youngster—yuck!"

"I'm sorry you don't like it," she said, "but I feel the *Eagle* has done us a great service. They waited a month in order to round up the latest archaeological news from all over the state. See, Bill? They've devoted four pages to our cause."

He didn't answer.

"Your comments are wonderful, Bill. I agree with what you said."

"You do?"

Aunt Cait put the paper on the floor beside her lounger. She got up and sat down at the foot of his. "What you felt that day is empathy."

She took hold of his ankle and squeezed gently. "Empathy is being able to walk in another person's shoes, see through their eyes, understand how they feel. Am I right, Bill? For a few moments at the dig, didn't you imagine you *were* that boy?"

"Yes," Bill said, "that's how I knew he didn't like being sacrificed. No kid would, not now and not back then either."

"I think you're right, Bill. Once you *know* you're part of the Great Spirit, you don't have to prove it *that* way."

"You mean you don't believe in sacrifices?" he asked.

"Not necessary," she answered. "You have a good

heart," she added. "The earth needs more links like you."

He'd been doodling in his notebook as she talked, and now he printed *EARTH*.

"Aunt Cait, look. If you take the last letter and put it first, *earth* spells *heart*. Isn't that something?"

12.

Glade of Light

Bill followed Annie from the wharf onto the flat-bottomed boat. "Wow, is this a hovercraft?"

"It's an airboat," Grant said, "or call it a sled with an eggbeater attached.

"You're right, though," he added, "at high speeds this contraption does hover. It has to. In some spots the water's only nine, ten inches deep.

"The coming storms should help bring the water levels up, but the sad truth is our *pahayokee* is drying up fast."

"Storms are coming?" Bill asked. "When?"

He definitely didn't want to be here in the Glades during a storm, not after hearing Grant's Manther tale.

Grant climbed up onto the high seat at the back of the boat. "Right about now, in August, we're at the peak of our wet season. Every afternoon, sometime after three, we'll get heavy rain for an hour or so. Then the clouds will move off to the west and the sun's shining again."

It was early, not yet eleven. Bill felt better. Probably they'd be long gone from here before any wet season started.

The air was humid, hanging still. The water around the airboat barely moved. It wasn't such a scary place, not as he'd imagined it'd be. Instead, the Glades seemed slow and dreamy, a good place to sit back and think about stuff. Even the little logs floating past the boat looked lazy.

"Oh, Bill, aren't they cute?" Annie pointed to the drifting logs.

"Sure, real cute." He laughed. "Hey, Annie, are you going to talk to logs like you do trees?"

If Annie answered him, Bill didn't hear her. Because one log, floating only a few feet from his side of the boat, blinked open a muddy-yellow eye.

It *yawned*.

Not a log—an alligator!

Man, that gator had to have at least a hundred jagged teeth with slimy spinach weeds stuck between them. Not that he wanted to count those bad teeth. Because if that log wasn't a log, Bill knew, those other logs weren't either!

As the noisy motor propelled the boat fast forward, the alligators turned. They slapped their tails, frothing up the brown water like a root-beer float in their rush to get away.

"That's it," he yelled, "keep going."

Grant slowed the boat's speed, and the fierce roar of the motor softened to a purr. Bill sat up straight and looked around.

On a small grass island ahead, he saw an orange and black butterfly make a perfect landing on the head of a wading stork. If he squinted behind his sunglasses, the bird looked like Needle Woman with a Halloween bow stuck to her silver hair.

"Hurry, Annie, get your camera." He pointed. "That's a prize-winner picture over there."

"Got it," Annie said. "Now, wait 'til you see mine." She handed over her binoculars.

When Bill aimed his magnified sights in the direction Annie pointed, he almost dropped the binoculars.

The spiderweb—like the one Grant had described in his Glades tale—stretched the size of a doubles volleyball net between two giant trees.

"Annie, the spider, it's bigger than a *mouse*! Hey, look, I think it's smiling at us, I think I see *teeth*!"

She raised her camera again. "Smile nice for the camera, Charlotte," she yelled. "Say *cheese*!"

"See that Spanish moss hanging on the mangroves?" Annie asked a few seconds later. "Calusa ladies used to make summer skirts from it. Calusa guys tied the moss to their backsides for portable cushions."

"Wouldn't catch me tying it to *my* backside!" he said. "That moss probably has all kinds of scorpions stuffed in it."

The giant mangroves bothered him. He remembered Annie telling him at the dig one day how black mangrove roots grew up and red mangrove roots grew down. She'd called the roots "knees."

But neither the up nor the down roots looked like knees to him. They looked like nasty witch fingers inching through the shallow water, inching closer to grab him. Vines looped over the mangroves' branches looked like they had the same idea. This place was beginning to give him the creeps.

Bill leaned forward. He sucked in a deep breath. Was *that* what he thought it was?

On that hummock over there, sticking out from behind the tree trunk, was a furry yellow tail! Man, Bill thought, the tail was even twitching back and forth.

A panther! Maybe *his* panther!

Swiveling on his seat, he held up his hand. Grant got the message and slowed the boat almost to a stop.

"Right there," he whispered, "a panther! Quick, Annie, the binoculars."

A minute later he handed them back. "It's only yellow flowers," he mumbled, "dumb yellow flowers crawling up the tree."

"Air plants," Annie explained. "All kinds of air plants grow here, even orchids. I love orchids, don't you?"

Bill stared down at his hightops.

"Won't see panthers here, Bill," Grant said. "During summer all fur animals head deep into the Glades, where it's cooler. We're not going that deep today, so don't get your hopes up.

"Not now, anyway. Thousands of years back Florida

had more kinds of roaming wildlife than Africa has today. We had rhinoceros, saber-toothed tigers, giant armadillos, huge dire wolves."

Grant laughed. "Even when I was a kid—just about your age—I'd be fishing here of an afternoon, and I'd swear ten thousand eyes were watching me.

"And was it ever noisy! The Glades hummed with life, a regular symphony of sounds. Swamp music, I called it. Now, unless I go in deep enough, I don't hear the songs anymore."

"I know another name for the Glades," Annie said.

"What is it?" Grant asked.

"*Glaed.* It's an old English word. My dad says Saxons and Viking explorers called this place Glaed. It means 'ever shining' or 'ever light.'" Annie sighed. "That's why Dad and I call it our Glade of Light."

Grant revved up the airboat after that and cruised the quiet waters without stopping. Bill hoped he was heading back to the wharf earlier than he'd planned. Maybe Grant smelled a rainstorm coming.

When he did stop the boat and climb down from his seat, it wasn't at the wharf. "This little hummock is a good place for our picnic," he said, "and after lunch I may get around to finishing the vision quest story."

Bill sat still, squinting up at the grassy mound. "Oh, sure," he croaked, "I can't wait for that great tale."

After lunch, when the sandwich papers and juice boxes were back in the covered picnic basket, he felt better. The only swamp creatures he'd spotted on this flat-topped hummock were a few tiny ants.

"So long as you both understand," Grant began, "that initiation rites may be different for each tribe or clan, each according to their own traditions.

"Understand, too, that for males and females the rites might be different. To make my story easier, I'll use a Calusa boy as my example."

He smiled. "So . . . without food, water, clothing, or weapons, the Calusa boy set off alone into the Glades. He went in search of his good medicine, a powerful animal spirit to guide and protect him through his life."

"The Calusa kid's parents let him go off like that," Bill asked, "bare-naked, with nothing to eat, without any weapon at all?"

"He carried his only important weapons here and here and here and here." Grant tapped his fingers at the center of his forehead, on each of his eyelids, at his heart and, last, at his gut.

"But you said, Aunt Cait said, the Glades can be dangerous, even if you know your way around. You just said, long ago the Glades had even more wild, dire animals. Didn't Calusas care about their kids getting clawed or chewed or eaten to death?"

"They cared that the boy learn about himself, that he discover his true nature, his weaknesses *and* his strengths."

Bill still didn't like it. "Couldn't he find out all that some other way? Wasn't the kid scared to go?"

"You said you wanted to hear this story," Annie interrupted, "and I do too, so—shhh."

"I don't mind questions," Grant said. "All right, now, before he left home, the boy fasted and purified his body in the sweat lodge. He prepared his mind with prayers and with the final instructions of his elders.

"Once in the Glades, he walked the trails he knew, but as he walked he looked for a place to break his own new trail. Once he was on his new path, he'd search for a high place to seek his vision."

Grant swept his strong coppery hand above his head. "This mound where we're sitting now might've been a good choice for his sacred circle. Up here he could see the cloud pictures, catch the eye of the sun, and listen to the wind messages."

"Sacred circle? What's that?" Bill asked.

Grant pointed to his shell earring. "See the cross in a circle? It's an ancient symbol of the Great Spirit and the four forces and directions of being."

"That's what Aunt Cait says too," Bill said. "She says the Great Spirit is everything we can think of all connected together: humans, animals, birds, fish, trees, shells, the sun, moon, and stars, the sea, even a speck of sand."

"My dad says it that way too," Annie said softly.

"Yes, well, according to his belief in the Great Spirit, the Calusa boy takes great pains to draw his sacred circle in the earth.

"First he finds the center of the circle, which stands for the center of himself. Then he walks outward from that holy spot, marking the four directions of his being and his world: west, north, east, and south."

"Then what?" Bill got ready to shoot Annie a dirty look in case she dared "shhh" him again, but she didn't even look up. As Grant talked she drew in her notebook.

"From that moment on," Grant said, "within the boundaries of the circle, he will walk and chant. With all his energy he will ask for a sign. Night and day he will dance and sing his prayers. Listen:

"Heee-ay, hay-eee,
Heee-ay, heee-ay, hay-eee—"

The strange chanting voice didn't sound at all like Grant's regular voice, and the words he sang were in a different language.

"Grant, you said night and day? How long does it take to get a vision, anyway?"

"It takes," he answered, "as long as it takes.

"Oh, the boy will be hungry, thirsty, sore, and afraid. But if he falls down from exhaustion and sinks into sleep, he will still use his dreams to seek his vision."

"What happened if the kid fell asleep so deep he forgot to have a prayer-dream? Or could he ever stop trying on purpose, you know—give up?"

"At every moment he has a choice," Grant said. "He can give up his quest or hang on awhile longer. But if he chooses to go on, then even when he can barely stand or keep his eyes open, he will keep trying. He will walk and pray and show his gratitude to the Great Spirit."

"Aunt Cait does gratitude," Bill said, "only *she* whispers."

"Yes, at times the seeker must stay quiet," he said. "He must listen hard to hear the approach first of the messenger animal, then, later, of his good medicine animal. He must be quiet within himself to see and hear the voice and the name of his own new power."

"If *I* was a Calusa, I'd be a medicine woman by now," Annie said. "I'd have a whole Glades pharmacy. No one would ever dare yell at me or throw my remedies and potions away in the dumpster. I'd have a big pot for cooking up stuff anytime I wanted."

"Phew, Annie, you would." Bill grinned. "You'd probably be boiling up all kinds of stinky fish and herb junk every day of the week."

Grant laughed too, then continued. "Whatever animal follows the messenger, whether it is in a waking vision or a dream, will be his power for life. He will take the animal's name as his own secret name.

"It could be that his spirit animal is a wolf, a bear, a panther, an alligator, or—"

"But, Grant, what if a regular animal didn't show up?" Bill asked. "What if just an *ant* showed up? Would his name have to be Ant?"

"I know a kid named Cricket," Annie offered.

"That's nothing," Bill said, "I know an ant—Aunt Cait!"

"Calusas respected the ant," Grant said, "as a hard-working and patient tiller of the soil."

When Grant stood up and stretched, Bill knew the tale was over, but he had another question. "Did King Calos have to cry for a vision? Maybe, since he was royal, he got out of doing it?"

"I imagine *because* he was royalty, he would have followed tradition to set a good example," Grant said.

"*You* didn't have to do it, did you, Grant? I mean, by the time you were a kid, all that stuff was out of style, right?"

"Seeking self-knowledge will never go out of style, Bill," he said. "And today the quest for inner power and confidence is going on stronger than ever before.

"And, yes, I did have to do it. I cried for my vision and found out who I truly am."

Staring up at Grant's strong, serious face, Bill asked one last question. "And who *are* you?"

"That," he said, "is my secret. When you learn the name of your guide, you keep it to yourself. Enough that you know. Not telling increases your power, do you see that, Bill?"

"I think so."

But he didn't see, not really. *Man,* Bill thought, *if I had a power name in* my *holy center, I'd shout it out!*

13.

Night with Needle Woman

"Bill?" Annie's voice carried clearly along the hall to the art gallery. "Hurry. Maggie's looking for you, and guess what. Grandma came early to pick us up. She's taking us somewhere—a surprise."

"Be right there," he answered.

"Bye, Your Highness," he whispered to the portrait. "It's been great communing with you."

For the final half hour of the last class, Bill had raced to finish two shell headbands. He had helped Mrs. Webster bore holes in three more shells. And when class had ended, saying good-bye to Maggie and the other students had taken so much time, Annie practically had to drag him away.

"Syl-via's sur-prise," she hissed now. "Come *on*, Bill."

"My treat, children—sweets for the sweet," Grandma Sylvia announced after they were settled in the backseat of her silver Buick. "To celebrate your accomplishments I'm taking you to the old Collier House."

"Why is she taking us to an old house?" Bill whispered.

"Oh, and don't worry, William, I phoned your great-aunt and informed her of our plans."

"The Collier House is *so* cool," Annie said. "You'll like it. It's over a hundred years old, but it looks brand-new."

He *did* like it. All lit up, with the big buildings of the Riverside Club looming behind it, the little house reminded him of his dwarf queen conch shell: It shone with importance.

Another thing he liked about the Collier House: It was an ice cream parlor!

On the front porch Bill wanted to stop and look at the giant carved-wood Calusa chief, but Needle Woman rushed them inside to an empty table. He and Annie sat down, but she didn't.

"I'm off to the powder room," she said. "While I'm gone, Vivianne, why don't you and your little friend decide what you'll have. Look at all those marvelous ice cream flavors. Every one delectable, I'm sure."

"Yes, Grandma," Annie said.

The second she was out of sight, Bill slumped forward onto the marble table. He almost bumped heads with Annie, who'd done the same thing.

"She's something else! I shouldn't say this, Annie, but—"

"But how do I stand her?"

"How *do* you?"

"Easy," she said. "When I'm with Grandma, I pretend I'm a marshmallow, not a real person. It makes her feel better. If you see a mooshy-looking kid eating ice cream later, don't think it's me."

"If you see that mooshy kid's *little friend*, don't think it's me, okay?"

"Deal. Let's make our delectable choices before she gets back. Look up there; besides all kinds of homemade ice cream, we could order truffles from Texas or—"

He read from the menu on the wall. "Pastries from Italy or black or white chocolate mouse cake or—"

"*Mousse* cake, not mouse," she said. "How about candy instead: macadamia brags or almond toffee or jelly bellies or—"

"There, now, children, have you decided?"

"Yes, Grandma, I'm having vanilla with hot fudge."

"Me too," Bill said.

"Marvelous. Would either of you like whipped cream? Chopped walnuts? Marshmallow?"

Bill put his face muscles on freeze-stop. If Annie even looked at him—

"Marshmallow for me," Annie said, "*lots* of marshmallow."

"Just fudge, Mrs. Stokes," he answered.

Tap-tapping her high heels across the floor tiles, she headed for the counter to place their orders. Annie sat back in her chair.

"I *know* you want to hear about Captain Bill Collier,"

she said. "Captain Bill built this house. His parents were Marco Island's first white settlers and—"

"So?"

"So Captain Bill helped discover the Key Marco Cat-god."

"No lie?"

"No lie. Way back in 1895 Captain Bill was digging up muck from a big mound near his house. He wanted to plant fruit trees, and the mound muck was great fertilizer.

"Anyway, Captain Bill started digging and—*klunk!*—his shovel hit something. He kept digging and—*klunk!*—it happened again and —*klunk!*—again—"

"Annie, stop klunking and get to the cat-god part."

"Well, the first klunk turned out to be ancient fishnet, and the second klunk was a beautiful conch shell cup, and the third klunk was two pieces of carved wood."

"The cat-god!"

"Not yet. Captain Bill kept digging up stuff. Pretty soon, he decided he was onto something important and ancient. So what did he do?"

"You're telling the story, not me."

"He called in the experts, that's what. It was a guy named Frank Hamilton Cushing who actually found the cat-god a year later. But if it hadn't been for the captain's klunking—"

"Vivianne? William? I need help here."

Bill shoved back his chair and shuffled his hightops

to the rescue. "Let me, Mrs. Stokes," he said in his deepest voice.

He set one heavy glass dish on the table in front of Annie and another dish at Needle Woman's place.

"Here's yours, William," she said, handing him his dish.

Bill took it, but with his free hand he pulled out her chair. She sat. "What marvelous manners you have, William!"

"Anyway," Annie continued, "the Key Marco Cat-god was dug up across this street."

"Now, let me set my handbag under here, out of the way."

Needle Woman's head disappeared beneath the table. He felt her stiff hairdo crowd against his knee-cap.

"Across *this* street?" Bill turned to look out the front window. *"Where?"*

"Look out, Bill!"

"I *am* looking out!"

But when he glanced back at her, Annie wasn't paying attention. Too late he saw why. His ice cream dish had tipped to one side. The fudge oozed—*glop, glop, glop*—onto Needle Woman's silver head.

And she didn't even know it yet!

She straightened, fixed her napkin on her lap, and daintily picked up her spoon. "Please, children, eat your sundaes. This is *your* party, your special treat."

Bill sank down into his chair. He checked to see what was left of his fudge. Not much.

Annie sat dead still, her spoon frozen in midair.

He stole another look at Needle Woman. Man! The fudge sludge was slowly . . . slowly . . . slip-sliding from the top of her hair toward the front.

Any second now, he knew, the fudge would slide over the falls of her bangs smack onto her face!

"Grandma?" Annie whispered.

"Mmm, yum!"

"Grandma!"

"Mmm, what?"

"Your hair, Grandma. You seem to have a . . . smudge of fudge on your hair."

"Fudge? A smudge? *My* hair?"

"More like a spill," Bill admitted. "Pretty massive."

She reached up, touched the pool of fudge, dabbling two fingers in it as if she were testing bath water.

Right then he wanted to crawl under the table next to her handbag.

"Argh," she gurgled, "argh, not again!"

Right then the fudge sludge broke loose. It cascaded down her hair to splatter on her cheeks. A separate fudge glob skied down her nose, landed in the groove underneath, and from there plopped onto her tongue.

"Argh . . . phfooey . . . phfft!" Sylvia sprayed fudge over her blouse, over the marble tabletop, over everything.

"Help Don't just sit there! Do something! Do something!"

"Grandma, take it easy. Here's napkins, here's water, here's—wait, I'll think of something, don't worry. I'll—"

"Never mind!" Grabbing her handbag from the floor,

Needle Woman hurried away from the table toward the powder room.

Don't worry? Bill thought. Soon, when Needle Woman got herself defudged, she'd figure out what had happened. Her needlefinger would point straight at him!

Annie's face was bright red. Bill heard weird sounds coming from her. Was she crying? he wondered. No, she was trying hard not to, but she kept doing it anyway. She was *laughing!*

"Sweets, Bill," she gasped, "sweets for the sweet, get it?"

He got it. And no matter what might happen next, Bill laughed too. "My treat," he said.

But when Sylvia didn't return he could see Annie getting nervous. She fidgeted with her napkin, with her spoon, then nibbled on her thumbnail.

"Maybe I should go see," Annie said. "What if she went home?"

"Take it easy," he said. "If she's gone, I'll phone my aunt. She'll come get us."

"I'll go see," she whispered. Annie got up and headed for the powder room.

More minutes passed. Bill worried. He guessed he'd better get it over with, find a phone and call Aunt Cait. She—

That's when he saw them coming toward him: Annie and a slim red-haired woman in a polka-dotted blouse. Watching them, Bill wondered why Annie would be holding hands with a stranger. Unless—

The woman *had* to be her mother. Sure, Annie's mother, come all the way from Paris, France. A regular *miracle!*

But as Annie and her mother reached the table, he wasn't so sure. "Annie, is that—"

"Sit *down,* William," the woman whispered. "I've had enough attention for one evening, thank you."

"Mrs. Stokes? Is that *you?*"

Plunking down in the chair opposite him, she set her elbows on the table, resting her chin on her hands, the way Annie always did. "A Wild Woman, that's what I look like. Don't say I don't."

"You *don't,* Syl—Mrs. Stokes. You look *good!*"

"See, Grandma?" Annie said, shooting him a grateful look. "I told you so. You never needed that wig. I'm glad it got ruined."

"Your tinfoil was a *wig?* With such great red curls, why'd you want to look *stiff?*"

"Elegant," Grandma Sylvia said. "At my age elegance and silver hair is in. Besides, redheads are expected to be vivacious and daring. I'm not, I'm shy. I'm not the outdoor type either. The truth is, I'm not comfortable outdoors."

"Don't feel bad, I'm not either," Bill admitted.

"You know, you two are look-alikes," he added. "When you were walking over before, I thought you were Annie's mother. Only difference is—Hey, I've got a present for you, Mrs. Stokes. Exactly what you need. Put it on and you and Annie will be twins!"

"Mmmm, only difference is about fifty years."

She stared down at the headband. "So well made and pretty, but, oh, I couldn't *wear* it. I'd look bizarre! I'm too *old*."

Annie grinned. "You'll look mar-velous, Grandma, honest."

"You two—ganging up on me. Next, you'll have me calling you Annie."

"Ohhh, will you?"

"I might." Grandma Sylvia bent her head. "Go ahead, Bill, put that Calusa thing on me. Who knows, maybe it will make a new woman of me."

14.

Ready or Not!

From the dinghy Bill watched Annie. She paced, kicking up sand behind her like a one-girl beach erosion.

"Grant will kill you if you take his boat out," she yelled.

He laughed. "Wrong, Annie. He's against extinction."

"Rain's coming," she screamed. "See those black clouds?"

"*Never* rains 'til after three."

"Bill, listen. The wind's picking up, feel it? If you get caught in the undertow—"

"Trade winds, Annie. Same as every day."

She did look scared, though. For a second he felt bad about teasing her. But not bad enough. It was fun sitting in the dinghy, fun pretending he meant to row all the way to the sandbar. What Annie didn't know was, he'd never *dare* do it.

Okay, since you don't want to come," he shouted, "I'm going now."

"Bill, *don't*. Bring the dinghy in now or . . . I'll *tell!*"

His grin faded. All summer, watching Annie and Grant row, he'd been dying to try it. Now that he almost had the hang of rowing, she wanted to ruin it for him.

Couldn't she see he was being extracareful to keep close to shore? Working the oars wasn't so hard. If he could practice more without her being such a brat about it, he might even know how to row by the time he went home next week.

But if she was going to tell, he'd better quit.

Bill dipped his left oar in the water and pulled hard. Good, the dinghy turned; all he had to do now was heave back hard on both oars to bring the boat to the beach.

It didn't work. Since the boat faced the wrong way, the beach was now farther away. "Hey, Annie," Bill yelled.

He saw her racing across the sand toward the path, and then she was gone, the high bushes and trees blocking her from his sight. Gone, just when he needed her most.

Bill tried again. And again. The hard part was keeping a strong-enough grip on the oars. He had the weird feeling the water was teasing him, trying to grab the oars out of his hands. His crazy imagination again, he knew. Seawater wasn't alive, part of the Great Spirit, no matter what Aunt Cait said.

The wind *was* stronger. It whipped his hair spikes backward and pressed the sunglasses hard against his face. It hurt.

And—man!—there was the sandbar, far over to his right. How'd that happen? The dinghy sped forward no matter what he did. It was as if giant magnets were sucking the little boat up like a paper clip.

His sunglasses were killing him, and they were so clouded over, he could barely see. Everything around him looked blurry and dark gray.

No! He should never have tried holding onto the oar and yanking his glasses off at the same time. That oar disappeared over the side so fast, he couldn't believe it.

Bill shivered. Holding tightly to his lone oar, he shielded his eyes with his free hand, straining to see the shore behind him. He could make out the sharp-angled shape of Horr's Island but where the beach should've been, there was only a blurred white line.

Grant's *Marco Polo* was already behind him. The dinghy practically flew over the choppy water. *"Help! Somebody help me!"*

His answer was thunder. Another crash came right afterward.

It was getting darker fast, wetter too; it felt like—
"Oh, no, please," Bill yelled, "don't rain yet!"

The wet gloom all around him was suddenly ripped to shreds by a huge jagged dagger of light. Not one dagger either but a whole series of them, as if, one after another, a team of knife throwers were out to get him.

"Aunt Cait—help!"

More deafening booms of thunder drowned out his yells. Another all-out attack of zigzagging bolts pierced the waves around him.

Lifting the oar from the lock, Bill struggled to stow it beneath the wooden seats. It wasn't doing him any good now, but he sure didn't want to lose it.

When the storm clouds burst their seams and dumped water all over him, he could only gasp and hunker over, covering his head with his arms.

The rain came down with such force, in thick, solid sheets, Bill cringed and cried out; he never knew rain could bomb down like this, hurting, beating at him hard.

"Help me!"

On his hands and knees, he tried to hold himself steady as the tiny boat shot ahead or spun dizzyingly sideways. The dinghy shuddered and creaked as the sea crashed against its sides. Beneath him the sea *did* feel alive and angry, like a raving maniac.

Blinded by the rain, deafened by the wind, Bill tried concentrating on the steady beat of the sea, but he couldn't.

The boat pitched forward and back, forward and back, then rocked on its side. It took every bit of his strength to keep himself on his hands and knees. He felt himself panicking.

Concentrate! Start counting!

Bill began to sob. *I'm going to drown*, he thought.

A wave hit the boat broadside, knocking him over, ramming his head against the side. He sprawled face up, dazed. Rain poured down on his eyelids, his nose, into his open mouth. It was the cold rainwater pouring down his throat that made him sit up, choking and gasping.

The dinghy was filling up fast; the water was already up over his wrists and ankles and rising every second. One thing he did know, if he didn't start bailing, he'd be dead!

Clinging with one hand to the wooden seat, Bill scooped water with his cupped hand. He needed something bigger. Nothing in his backpack was big enough. That's when the good idea hit him: He'd use one of his hightops for a bailing bucket!

He stopped crying. Crying wasn't helping much, and he needed all his energy for the job ahead.

"One," Bill yelled against the wind, "two ... three ..."

Over and over he dunked his hightop under the water in the boat, waited until it filled up, then tossed the water overboard.

Counting as he bailed did help. Pretending he was a robot helped too. He knew he couldn't stop bailing even for a minute. The water in the bottom of the boat kept rising.

The storm around him was worse: thick, cold rain clubbing his head and shoulders, the wind shrieking, thunder booming, lightning flashing through the fog.

Barely able to see his robot hand with the hightop attached, Bill handled his fear in the only way he could: "One ... two ... three."

When the rain slowed and clumps of green appeared

through the tattered shreds of fog, he saw—
hummocks! Everywhere he looked he saw small mangrove islands. He knew every one had to be crammed
with deadly creatures.

The storm had swept him through the Gateway into
the Glades. He remembered Aunt Cait saying how
even old experienced sailors got lost out here. Now he
was lost too, and the wind and the current were taking
him where he definitely didn't want to go. Every
minute the dinghy was moving deeper and deeper into
the Ten Thousand Islands maze.

Sitting there, his robot arm halted in midair over
the edge of the boat, Bill felt like crying again. He was
tired and wet all over, but what worried him most was
knowing what he'd have to do.

If he didn't want to go any deeper into the maze,
he'd have to get near enough to one of those hummocks
to wade or swim ashore. If he didn't, no one would ever
catch up to him. *But how*, he wondered? *How can I do
it with only one oar? Impossible . . .*

The rain had turned to drizzle, the wind only a
cranky whine, and the sheets of sea had stopped rushing so fast.

Boom! The dinghy lurched hard, his hightop slipping from his numb fingers into the water.

Oh, no! As fast as he could, Bill dangled his arm over
the side of the boat, trying to grab his hightop before it
went underwater. Instead . . . instead he grabbed
something slick and solid, something with *muscle
tone*!

Snatching his head away, he craned his neck for a look.

Sharks!

Not just a couple of sharks, a whole crowding-close gang of them!

Man, he'd never even thought of sharks.

Bad enough to think about getting jawed to death, shaved into little pieces by all those razor teeth. What was making it worse, they were taking their time about it, teasing him, nudging the dinghy back and forth.

Trembling, Bill curled himself into a tight body ball on the bottom of the boat, waiting for the End.

"Click-click! Click-click-click!"

He opened his eyes, Aunt Cait's words loud in his mind. *"Click-click-click* in Dolphinese means "Wanna ride?"

Dolphins? Instead of sharks? Could it possibly be?

"Click!"

Holding his breath, Bill peeked over the side of the boat and saw—poking its head way up out of the water beside the dinghy—a medium-sized dolphin smiling right at him.

He sat up fast. "Hi, buddy. Wow, am I ever glad to see you." Bill sighed. "I'm in big trouble. I'm lost out here—bad!"

The dolphin raised itself almost all the way out of the water, balancing on its tail, watching him from one round curious eye.

"I guess you already know that, huh?"

The dolphin's smile and steady, beaming gaze were friendly and, at the same time, sympathetic. It was the weirdest thought he'd ever had, but this dolphin reminded him of Aunt Cait. So many times she'd looked at him, smiled at him, in exactly the same way.

"See, I'm trying to get over to that—"

Astonished, Bill stared around him. The dinghy was pointed straight toward an open space between two green-tangled arms of land. The dolphins had read his mind!

"Guess you knew that too, right?"

But his dolphin was already back in the water, peeling away from the boat, power-swimming through the water to join up with his big family.

From the boat Bill watched them playing, leaping from the water in pairs, crisscrossing each other in midair, diving down, jumping up again. He could hear them too. He'd never realized dolphins were so conversational; their high-pitched clicks, chirps, and whistles mixed with all their water splashing sounded like a swimming party.

But when the dolphins disappeared, his warm, tingly connected feeling disappeared too. He felt worse, colder, lonelier, more afraid.

The dinghy drifted into the outstretched green arms of the hummock. In the shadowy brown water he saw mangrove roots, gnarled and knobby-knuckled. Witch fingers! The worst he'd ever seen. If he had to sit in the boat all night, he'd do it, Bill decided. Even in the pitch-darkness he'd be better off.

He thought of Grant's love-sick alligator story. Maybe he *wouldn't* be better off hanging out all night in this boat.

"*Ouch!* Hey—*ouch!*"

A cloud of mosquitoes covered him, biting every piece of his skin, flying up his nostrils, biting behind his ears, biting everywhere. Bill couldn't stand it. Not like any New Jersey mosquitoes he'd ever known; these were killer mosquitoes.

"Ow—get off me—*help!*"

The mosquitoes made him choose fast. He grabbed up his backpack, put it on, then got a good grip on the oar. He knew he'd need the oar to pole himself closer in to the shore.

As soon as he got the dinghy close enough to a branch, Bill grabbed for it with one hand and caught it. He hung on, letting his foot dangle down to search for a solid place to stand.

There! His foot found a place and— "*Ow! Get off— ow!*"

Hanging from the branch with one hand, he squirmed and twisted his body while he kicked and hit at the mosquitoes with the oar.

No! He'd kicked the dinghy away! Over his shoulder he watched it drift slowly across the quiet lagoon. But he couldn't watch long; the mosquitoes were all over him. He *had* to find a foothold.

At last Bill got one foot, then the other onto a wide, strong root. From there he leapt to a shelf of spongy moss. All he knew was to keep moving, to reach higher ground, away from the bugs and snakes.

But climbing up through the thickets of leaves and vines wasn't going to be easy. Cautiously Bill poked the oar past the outer layer of dappled yellow and green mangrove leaves. He pushed forward through the green opening.

He wished Annie were here right now. She'd talk their way up through the vines and sticker bushes, past any dire creature lurking in there.

"Excuse me, please," Bill whispered to the giant leaves ahead. "Can I come in? I'm from New Jersey and I'm lost and, hey—I don't mean you any harm."

15.

Where Cat-gods Cry

"If you ever find yourself in a bad situation, concentrate on another idea or emotion. Focus your mind and presto—"

Crouched on the ground next to his backpack, Bill groaned.

Presto nothing! Anyway, easy for Grant to say. For Aunt Cait too. Neither of them could ever be as scared as he was right now. Grant and Aunt Cait were adults; they'd know exactly what to do to save themselves.

What could *he* do? Focusing his mind wouldn't help if an alligator or a deadly snake decided to have him for supper.

It'd be different if he'd been born to the Glades, like Grant or a Calusa kid. If he was a Calusa kid, he might even like being atop a mound in the middle of a mangrove maze. If he was a Calusa kid crying for a vision, he probably wouldn't mind being hungry, thirsty, and falling-down dizzy.

Still, he had to do *something*. If he could concentrate on doing a vision quest, maybe he'd forget being terrified. If he could remember enough of what Grant had said that day in the Glades, maybe the Great Spirit would hear and help him make it through the long night ahead.

Was there a Great Spirit? He hoped so. He needed all the help he could get.

From his position high on the mound, Bill saw that the sun had already set. Dying embers of red light flared along the horizon, but everything else—the sea, the sky, the tangled vines and bushes, and the mangrove leaves hanging overhead—had turned dusky purple.

On the ground too, blue shadows crept in closer and closer. In minutes, he knew, it would be dark. Later—*pitch*-dark.

Bill leapt to his feet.

First, as fast as he could, he outlined the circle with bits of broken oyster shells he found heaped beyond the clearing. He marked out the four directions, using the sun's position as his guide for west to east.

Just let any creature try sneaking into his ceremonial circle during the night. He'd hear the shells rattling and—

Just thinking about it gave him the creeps.

Next, with vines, he tied Manther to the paddle-end of the oar. Planting the other end in the sandy soil, he mounded shells around it to hold it steady and straight. With the cat-god attached, the oar looked authentic Calusa and—sort of—sacred.

Bill strained to remember more of what Grant had told him that day.

From that moment on, within the boundaries of the circle, he will walk and chant.

Starting off from the Sacred Oar, Bill walked west, stopping at the shell barrier. He held out his arms to the purple sky as he'd seen Grant do. Returning to the oar in a careful heel-to-toe line, he repeated his walk south, east, north, and west again.

Night and day he will sing his prayers.

That was the hard part. Walking the circle was one thing, but praying? What could he say? "Excuse me, Great Spirit, but I'm from New Jersey and I'm lost." No, he couldn't say *that* again—much less sing it.

Walk! From this moment on walk without ceasing. Pray for a sign. Open your heart and send your song to the Great Spirit of All There Is.

The words were no longer Grant's. The voice was calm and quiet, and it seemed to come from somewhere deep inside Bill himself.

"*Heee-ay,*" Bill chanted, "*hay-eeeeeee!*" He hadn't understood one word of what Grant sang; he wished now he'd asked him to translate the strange prayer-song.

A Calusa kid would know all kinds of prayer-songs. Before he set out on his vision quest, a Calusa kid got sweated-out in a lodge and instructed by his elders.

Aunt Cait was an elder, but what good were the instructions she'd given him? Thank you notes, that's all she'd said about praying. But thank yous were for when the Great Spirit gave you gifts to be glad about.

Was he supposed to say "Thanks, Great Spirit, for giving me such great wind and rain, lightning and thunder? Thanks a lot for tossing me over the waves smack into this marvelous mangrove maze?

"Mostly, Great Spirit, thanks for your nice mosquitoes, and your cute little strangler vines and mangrove roots. Your *spectacular* sunset too; it was great while it lasted."

Walk, don't think—pray!

But he couldn't. In the thickening shadows all he could do was stand, straining his eyes to see. His eyes burned, and he heard a strange buzzing in his ears. With the sun gone he felt cold.

Crouching again, Bill unsnapped his backpack and pulled out the neatly folded King Calos cape. A few minutes later, huddled within the soft, warm cloth, Bill thought about all the times he'd played at being the mighty cacique. Then he'd been safe and sound in his room with the door closed. Way up here in the wild darkness, it was hard to pretend, too hard to imagine himself as a mighty anything. He was scared, that's all, and so tired and weak his eyelids wouldn't stay up.

Sighing, he rummaged through his pack until he found the flashlight Aunt Cait had lent him. If the flashlight gave off even a dim light, he'd be lucky. More than lucky, he decided. He'd been using the flashlight practically every night these past few weeks.

If only he hadn't sucked all the juice out of the batteries pretending the flashlight was a Calusa torch.

If only he hadn't even come to Marco Island with Aunt Cait and caught her Calusa craziness.

If only he hadn't done a lot of things, he'd be okay right now. Mostly, Bill thought, if only I'd listened to Annie.

He wondered what Annie would think if she could smell him right now. He'd used her bug oil; it was great stuff. It kept the mosquitoes away and took the sting out of the bites he already had.

If only—

Too late for if only*'s. Walk!*

Reeking of the smelly oil of fish, Bill wrapped the shell-studded cape closer around him. With the cape to protect his skin from scorpions and other biting bugs, maybe he could take a break, close his eyes, sleep awhile. Sleep, that's what he needed.

When Bill opened his eyes again, he was relieved to see bright moonlight shining into his circle of shells. Because, outside the moonlit circle, it was jet-black. It was noisy out there too. So many noises: screeches and scratchings, eerie chitterings and twitterings. The bushes around him and the treetops above were alive with awful sounds, rustlings and whirrings and weird whisperings.

So that's what Grant called swamp music; he could have it!

Bill stood, reaching up to slide Manther from his bindings at the top of the Sacred Oar. The little statue felt good in his hands, solid and silky and cool. "Listen!" he whispered in the cat-god's ear. "Think *that's* not scary for a kid?

"In your day, this four-direction circle was sacred, right? Take that word *sacred*, take the *a* and *c*, slip your tongue wrong for a second, and what do you get? *Scared*, that's what—a scared circle!"

Bill shivered in the cool night air. "Sorry," he added. "I forgot you don't have a tongue. I wish you did. I wish you had claws and fangs too. I could use a real live Florida panther right now. If you were alive, you could prowl outside this circle for me, keep watch until rescue comes."

He heard a loud rustling in the bushes beyond the shell barrier. "What's that?"

Close by in the swirling blackness, something moved. Straining his eyes, Bill could see it lurching toward him. Grabbing up the flashlight, he pushed at the switch. All he could make out in the faint glare was a squat, hulking shape—a dwarf!

A dwarf masked bandit!

Wait! A dwarf *two-headed* masked bandit—with *four arms*! Trembling, Bill held the cat-god statue out in front of him.

"Hold it," he croaked. "Don't make another move or I'll shoot."

But the freak-of-nature bandit *did* move. On four feet he stepped into the edge of the moon spotlight.

Bill burst out laughing.

"Manther, look," he gasped, "raccoons—*twins*."

But before he could hold the cat-god upright again

for a good look, the raccoons whirled, twitched their bushy black-ringed tails, and were gone from his sight, crashing back through the bushes.

Hey, Bill wondered, *could those raccoons be twin messenger signs? A doubleheader?* Wrapping the cape around himself again, he sat down on the ground to think about it.

A minute later he heard shells rattling—*chink-chink*.

Bill jerked his head around just in time to see a little gray armored tank crashing over the shell barrier.

Fighting free of the cape, he leapt to his feet, racing to the opposite edge of the circle. Bill kept out of its way, until he spotted something he hadn't noticed before: a *tail*.

An armadillo! A regular nine-banded armadillo, in real life even weirder than in the photograph in one of Aunt Cait's nature books.

Not soon enough, the confused creature crashed through another section of shells, scrabbling and scuttling away into the darkness.

Bill was confused too. Could the armadillo be another messenger animal? Or—he hoped not—could it be his actual good medicine animal? Grant had said there would be only one messenger animal.

"Maybe the racoons weren't a sign after all," he said. "Maybe the armadillo was the— Manther, where *are* you?"

He knew he'd been holding him before he'd jumped up. Manther had to be here, he couldn't be gone. But if the cat-god had fallen outside the circle, Bill knew he'd never be able to find him in the dark, not with this weak flashlight.

After walking the circle five times, peering into the darkness and listening to the silence, he gave up. But why was it quiet? A cold feeling slid along his spine. What was wrong?

The answer to his question came rumbling through the shadows. Bill froze. He'd recognize that bad bronchitis cough anywhere.

It *couldn't* be Manther. No matter what the ancient Calusas believed, a little carved cat statue—especially a copy of a statue—could never come to real life, not in fifty thousand years.

Never! It couldn't happen, not today, not in this world.

Which meant a live, wild Florida panther was out there in the dark.

There it was again, that deep-down, growly give-away cough.

Bill wrapped his arms around himself and pulled tight. What would he ever do if the panther padded into the circle, white fangs gleaming, curving needle claws ready to snatch him?

Oh! Straight ahead, looking right at him, were two glowing yellow-stone eyes.

"Manther," he whispered, "please—you sure that's not you out there?"

He was shaking. "Help, please," he whispered hoarsely. "If you hear me, Great Spirit, I wish you'd tell me what to do. See, the trouble is, I'm pretty small for my age."

"*Grrrrr . . .*"

"Huh?" Bill stepped backward until his heels hit the oar. "Did you say something, Great Spirit? See, I'm *really* scared right now, stark terrified if you'd like to know. A kid like me, small and, well, wimpy, doesn't stand a chance out here in the wilderness."

Were the panther eyes still there? He checked. Yes.

"*You* make yourself small."

Whoa! Whose voice was that? The Great Spirit's? The panther's? Could this panther actually talk?

"Only if I have to."

"Excuse me, Great Spirit, is that you? I hope so, because I need advice in a hurry. There's a live panther roaming out there in the dark waiting to get me."

"Waiting for an invitation, Bill. It's entirely up to you."

An invitation? He shook his head. This had to be some kind of weird dream he was having.

"Whenever you're ready. Anytime you choose, you can take off your armor, throw away your masks, and invite your power in to stay."

"Who, me? Didn't you hear me? I'm small, that's all. It's not *my* fault. I was born that way."

Man, if the Great Spirit didn't understand about being an undersized runt, who ever would?

"Your panther understands loneliness. Listen—"

A scream, louder than any he'd ever heard, pierced the hushed night air. The scream rose higher, louder, climbing the unseen looping vines overhead, leaping from leafy treetop to leafy treetop.

Wailing through the night, the scream swooped into the shell circle, into him. Bill felt it in every part of his body. The scream vibrated in his ears, in his chest; it made his heart pound and his throat ache. It brought tears to his eyes.

Bill couldn't bear to hear it. It was a scream like no other, mournful, filled to the brim with longing and loneliness.

For as long as he lived, he knew he'd never be able to forget this haunting, heartbroken scream.

My panther? Can it possibly be?

"Don't cry," he whispered, "please, don't cry . . . I'm here."

But he was not through crying himself. Covering his hot, tear-stricken face with his hands, Bill sobbed for the lonely, sad, endangered panther. He sobbed for himself, lonely, sad, and endangered too.

As he sobbed, the small hole in his soul torn open by that piercing panther scream grew wider and wider, wide enough for something magnificent and golden and untamable to step in.

At last he wiped away his tears and firmed his shoulders. *If my panther came all this way just to be my good medicine, the least I can do is show some respect. Show some gratitude.*

Much later, with his back against the Sacred Oar, Bill sat cross-legged on the ground waiting for daybreak. White mist swarmed and swooped around him like mosquito-netting ghosts. He forced himself to think of the hovering misty forms as friendly Calusa spirits come to watch over him.

He felt the presence of another, stronger spirit. It didn't matter that he couldn't see his good medicine panther, he could hear. Faintly, every so often, the tell-tale noises filtered through the mist.

"*Pssst-shhh*" —the sound of cold water hitting red-hot coals.

"*Hagh-hagh-hagh*" —the bad bronchitis cough.

Mostly, though, Bill heard a smooth, steady car-motor purr. The sound of that contented purr made him feel less scared. He pictured the great tawny cat prowling silently, circling his ring of shells, keeping watch, keeping harm away.

"Thanks," Bill called softly into the dense, swirling fog, "I appreciate it."

He'd already decided, if he ever got to see Annie again, he'd ask her what a person who wanted to save panthers from extinction would be called. Bill guessed she'd come up with a couple of smart-sounding words. *Pantherologist* sounded good. If he could, if he got saved, that's what he'd be someday.

At times, though, he couldn't hold his focus. At those moments his mind drifted, and the doubts and panic crowded in. He wasn't sure if he was asleep or awake. Bill even wondered if he was still alive. Maybe a wild, deadly creature *had* come upon him while he dozed and eaten him for dinner.

Maybe this white cocoon mist was actually a cloud

floating high above the mangrove maze. Maybe he was time-traveling back to Calusa days. Maybe—

Concentrate. Focus. Don't panic.

To refocus his mind, Bill had only to touch his royal feathered turban or finger the triple-strand shell and feather necklace he wore around his neck. He'd forgotten exactly when during the long night he'd taken the turban and his collection of shell jewels from his pack, but wearing them gave him a safer, anchored feeling.

Best of all, he had Manther back. Bill had found the cat-god safe and sound, kneeling upright on the ground at the base of the oar—a regular miracle. To feel calmer inside, all he had to do was stroke the silky surface of the cypress wood.

Once he swore he heard Manther's small voice speaking to him: "Don't worry, I'm here, we'll think of something."

16.

Connected

From the top of the hummock Bill watched the Great Spirit sun rise on the eastern horizon. In just minutes, the cool gray morning came alive, shimmering with golden light. The water, the sky, the leaves and vines above his head, the flowering bushes beyond the circle—even the piles of broken shells—looked brand-new. He shoved the heavy cape back from his shoulders and let it fall to the ground. Already he was hot and every muscle in his body ached. Squinting against the glare of the sun, he stood on tiptoe, stretching his arms high above his head to get the kinks out.

Now what? he wondered. With the dinghy drifted away, and with ten thousand islands for Aunt Cait and Grant to search, Bill knew he had to come up with a way to help himself get saved. But how?

"Have no fear." The deep, mellow voice came from

behind him. "It's a new day. All things are possible."

Bill whirled. "Grant?" He looked again and felt his knees grow weak. "Oh, my gosh, King Calos, I don't believe it."

"Believe it, you'll see me."

He could see, all right. King Calos towered above him, his rich copper skin gleaming in the sunlight. Beneath his plumed turban his black eyes glistened.

Frantic, Bill pinched his own cheek. He scratched at a mosquito-bite welt on his wrist so hard he drew blood.

"I'm awake? I'm not imagining you?"

"Do I look imaginary?"

"No," Bill whispered, "you look—*big*."

"Indeed. Calusas were once giants on earth, fierce warriors, wise priests, and fine artists. But by the time the conquerers came, our grand empire was on the decline. Our hearts and minds were shrinking fast."

Bill kept his distance. "You mean, like the Glades? My friend Grant says once the *pahayokee* goes, part of us goes too."

"Too many times I forgot my true purpose on earth as I walked the chief's path." He sighed. "Ah, well, live and learn . . . die and learn."

"*Die* and learn?" On the sly, Bill pinched himself again.

"Exactly. As my spirit roams free, it remembers and grows large again."

"About sacrificing kids," Bill said, "it doesn't make sense. If you ask me, it's—"

"Not necessary," King Calos said. "At the time we only thought it was. We thought we needed all the help we could get. We were wrong."

"Oh," Bill said, glad to hear it. He took a baby step forward. "What really happened? Did *all* the Calusas go up in smoke overnight?"

"Not me. An arrow shot by a Spanish crossbowman caught me"—the king clutched his throat—"right here."

Excited, Bill reached into the pocket of his damp jeans and pulled out a stick of gum. It was precious, his last hope before starvation. He tore the stick in two and held out a half.

"No," the cacique said, "looks like good silver. Let's trade, your silver for mine."

That"—he pointed to the foil gum wrapping—"and that"—he pointed to the flashlight on the ground—"for this." Proudly he tapped his shining silver headband.

"Wow," Bill said, eyeing the cross-in-a-circle design etched on the silver, "a two-for-one sale! I have to tell you, Your Highness, I'm getting the better deal."

King Calos smiled. "I know, but I want you to have it. Trust me, for you it will shine far. One question, Bill, did your good medicine animal ever show up?"

"Oh." He looked away. "That. Well, it's secret, isn't it? It's supposed to be enough that I know, right?"

"Exactly right, which means, my work here is done. It's time for me to go."

"Don't go, Your Highness," Bill pleaded. If this *was* a

dream, he didn't want it to end. "You could stay with me awhile. Plenty of room, and I could use the company."

"Ah, then you do have room in your sacred circle for me?"

"Yes!"

"Then, it is done." In a single stride the king crossed the shell barrier. "We'll be good for each other," he said. "I'll help you walk tall, and I'll show you the wider view. I see a lot in my travels. I'll teach you."

"You will?"

"I promise," he said. "And your good medicine animal will also help. Depend on our power and great instincts."

"Whew! I could use some great instincts right now," Bill said. "Probably Aunt Cait won't find me in a million years unless I—"

"Unless you commune." The cacique came a giant step closer. "Send messages across the sky, across the water and— Here, let me help."

Before Bill could blink or even breathe, the door of his soul swung open wide again to admit one tall, great Calusa spirit: the king.

For a long time afterward he watched the sun slide higher. From where he stood the sun looked like a gigantic glowing panther eye. It made him feel good inside. It made him believe.

Below the hummock the waters flashed. Above him white feather clouds floated. Bill studied a pelican sky patrol riding the air currents, flapping their heavy bodies toward home.

Home? The birds were headed in the direction from which he'd come. He remembered Aunt Cait telling him Marco Island was the northern-most island of the Ten Thousand Islands' maze.

"Hey, pelicans, do me a favor, please? Drop a few feathers on my aunt's porch. Let her know I'm alive. Thanks!"

Yelling to the pelicans gave him another great idea, only for this message he guessed he'd use his mind, not his lungs.

Bill beamed his thoughts across the distance. "Dolphin? Buddy? If you hear me, and if you're not doing anything better right now, would you watch for the *Island Lady*? Point her in the right direction like you did for me? Thanks a lot!"

He thought of more friends to call: Annie, Aunt Cait, Grant, Grandma Sylvia, and Maggie.

He guessed he'd call Mom and Dad too. They couldn't help doing what they loved: traveling, the food business, meeting new people. If they'd sent him here to have a good time and to build up his self-confidence—well, it had worked, hadn't it?

No sense in calling Cory, Rob, or Stillman, Bill decided. They couldn't hurt him anymore, but they couldn't help him either. They didn't even know him— not yet.

Bill picked up the silver headband. As he held it up, sunbeams caught at its surface and bounced off again. "Ahhh!" Now he knew what the king meant by "for you it will shine far."

I'll make *it shine far*, he thought.

At the bottom of his backpack, Bill found the tube of lipstick Maggie had donated toward his Calos costume. For sun block, for luck, and for life, he smeared the greasy red goop all over his face.

Sparkles of golden light from the great panther eye bounced off the silver crown to flash northward. Bill counted under his breath slowly: "One, two, three . . . one, two, three."

The hours passed, the sky began to darken. Still, Bill kept shining, kept counting. As he did, he watched and listened for a sound, a sign—an answer.

The sun had only just set when he heard the familiar humming whine of the *Island Lady*'s motor. Over the whine he heard Annie's voice. *"Bill, Bill, where are you?"*

"I'm up here," he yelled.

He saw Annie waving like crazy. *"I see him! There he is!"*

Like crazy, Bill waved back. *"Wait, I'm coming down."*

As fast as he could he tossed his belongings into the backpack. The oar could stay. Maybe someday, he thought, another scared, lost kid might need it.

Heading downward through the tangled thickets of green, Bill made sure to tread carefully. He whispered all the way: "Let me pass, please? Thanks, I appreciate it. Good-bye . . . good-bye."

When he reached the narrow white-sand beach, Annie was already out of the boat and splashing through the shallows.

"Oh, Bill," she said, "you're alive!"

He grinned. "How can you tell, Annie?"

"Your face. That's for life, isn't it?" She laughed and ballet-leaped a circle around him.

"Guess what, Bill? Dolphins led us here. One dolphin, he was so funny, he—"

"I know who you mean. That's Buddy."

Annie insisted on carrying his backpack to the boat. "You look different," she said behind him. "I know, you're walking different."

"I am?"

Bill wished for a moment he could tell her the truth. He would've liked to say: "Listen, Annie, it's humanly impossible for a kid to get a Calusa king and a good medicine panther into his system overnight and *not* be different."

Aunt Cait reached out and yanked him out of the water into her arms. Her hug practically cracked his ribs apart. "After so many hours of searching," she told him, "I stopped at home to change clothes. I was standing on the porch waiting for Grant to pick me up when, not one, not two, but *three* pelican feathers floated down in front of me. Now, Bill, I'd have to have rocks in my head not to see those feathers as good omens. I knew then we'd find you, safe and sound."

Grandma Sylvia smacked a kiss on his smeary, smelly cheek and didn't even seem to mind it.

Grant's man-to-man hug set his ribs back in place again.

"We saw your mirror signals, Bill," he said. "Good thinking."

"Not a mirror, Grant—*this*." He pulled the silver crown from his pack and held it up for all to see.

The way Aunt Cait carried on Bill figured the head-band had to be important, maybe as important as the cat-god, the toy catamaran, and the mummy. In fact, she looked so enthusiastic, he guessed that if her wrinkles curved up any more than they already had, they'd become wings and take off flying.

She unfolded her nautical chart and uncapped her pen. "Here, I'll mark the location with an *X*." She looked up. "The hummock doesn't have a name. Why don't I mark it Bill Key?"

"Aunt Cait, I know a better name," he said, praying he wouldn't give away his secret.

"Call it Panther Glade. Only because it sounds good, and"—he patted the cat-god statue resting in his lap—"and sort of after him."

Aunt Cait smiled. "Forget *X*, that's what we'll call it: Panther Glade. I'll write it in big red letters."

Seated opposite him, Annie leaned forward, her eyes a brighter *glaed*-green than all the Ten Thousand Islands put together.

"I know a good name for *you*, Bill."

"What, Annie?" He really wanted to know.

"Brave," she said, "a good name for you is brave!"

About the Author

Helen Cavanagh always wanted to be a writer. Growing up in Newton, Massachusetts, at times she also wanted to be an explorer, an archaeologist, a naturalist, or, maybe, a medicine woman. All those early ambitions came true at once on Marco Island, as she researched and wrote *Panther Glade*, her eleventh book for young people.

Helen Cavanagh lives with her family in Spotswood, New Jersey.